# THE

# MINOT

# MISSION

## STEPHEN KNIGHT

*We at Trafford believe that it is the responsibility of us all, as both individuals
and corporations, to make choices that are environmentally and socially sound.
You, in turn, are supporting this responsible conduct each time you purchase a
Trafford book, or make use of our publishing services. To find out how you are
helping, please visit www.trafford.com/responsiblepublishing.html*

*Our mission is to efficiently provide the world's finest, most comprehensive
book publishing service, enabling every author to experience success.
To find out how to publish your book, your way, and have it available
worldwide, visit us online at www.trafford.com*

*Trafford rev. 01/07/2010*

 www.trafford.com

**North America & international**
toll-free: 1 888 232 4444 (USA & Canada)
phone: 250 383 6864 ♦ fax: 812 355 4082 ♦ email: info@trafford.com

*To my grandfather Cyril Knight*
*whose 1947 oil painting, Atomic Man,*
*was the inspiration for this book.*

## February 1982

Many beers had been drunk that night at the Thunderbird Motel across the road from the entrance to the local snow-covered fairgrounds. Mike and Larry Fuller staggered out of the motel's restaurant into the frigidly cold morning air. Almost at the same time, Wolford Byford's pickup truck screeched to a halt in front of them, its headlights momentarily blinding them. Larry opened the passenger door and the brothers scrambled up into the big pickup's cab. Wolf, as Byford was known, gunned the truck out of the icy motel parking lot, spitting up snow and gravel. On the radio, Bruce Springsteen was belting out his latest hit *Hungry Heart*. About a mile up the highway, Wolf turned north onto Foxhollow Road, screeching the tires as he took the bend too fast. The community of Foxhollow where they lived, was about ten miles north of where they were. Mike, the younger and drunker of the Fuller brothers, had passed out, resting his head on his brother's shoulder.

The snow banks along the side of the dark highway were unusually high. More snow than normal had fallen in the area since the beginning of the year. It must have been at least twenty below outside. Wolf could see his breath and his hands were getting cold. He was rubbing them together to try to warm them. Wolf asked Larry if he wanted a smoke and when he declined, lit one up himself, filling the cab with white drifting smoke. As they sped north, they were the only vehicle on the road on that bitterly cold night.

The flying saucer could easily be seen with the naked eye, although it took Wolf awhile to notice it. Even after seeing it, he didn't believe it. He figured it must be a reflection on the windshield and turned the pickup's headlights off, but the object could still be clearly seen. He pulled off the highway alongside a high snow bank, turned the radio off and said to Larry, "Look over there," pointing to the top of the windshield.

Larry tilted his head slightly and looking under the rear-view mirror, focused as best he could on what looked like a flying saucer, moving across the night sky.

"I see it!" he yelled excitedly and nudged his brother Mike until he came awake.

"What is it?" Mike asked. "Are we home?"

"Can you see it?" Larry asked. "Look over there."

Mike leaned forward and looked where Larry was pointing. Yawning, he said, "Yeah I see it, what is it, but now I can't see it no more."

They had all lost sight of the object behind the snow-covered trees along the side of the highway. Wolf pulled back onto the highway and it came back into view again. He was trying to figure out what it could be. It could be a plane coming into land at the nearby Air Force base; then again it might have just taken off, but it seemed to be heading towards the base rather than away from it. He lost sight of it again.

The trip home had passed very quickly thanks to the strange object; they were already passing an old abandoned farmhouse on the outskirts of Foxhollow. Another few minutes and Wolf would be dropping the Fullers off. As he turned into the street where they lived, the object came into view again, but a moment later disappeared behind one of the huge elms that had originally given the street its name. Wolf stopped in front of the Fullers' house, and shouted "You're home."

Larry struggled with the passenger door, pushed his brother out and followed after him, landing on top of him on the snow-covered boulevard. Wolf could see the brothers pushing each other as he stretched across and pulled the passenger door shut. He drove off and in his rear-view mirror could still see the Fullers lying in a heap in front of their house.

Wolf was of two minds what to do. He could go home and put the incident down to a case of being disoriented due to having drunk too much, or he could try to find if the mysterious object was for real. He thought that since the Fullers had seen it too, it must be real. He checked his watch; it was twenty-five minutes after three. He sped through the back roads between Foxhollow and the local Air Force base, driving as fast as he could, the back end of his truck fish tailing from side to side as he flew around tight bends leaving clouds of swirling snow behind him. He just hoped he didn't run into a base security patrol, because it would be difficult to explain what he was doing out here, at that time in the morning. As he came out of the trees into a clearing, he could see the object high in the sky, circling above the northern base perimeter road. He was beginning to have second thoughts about finding out what it was, when he saw two parachutes open up against the night sky.

# CHAPTER 1

## Soviet Union - February 1981

Deep in the bowels of a building within the walls of the Kremlin, a Soviet general was sitting in a deserted meeting room. He was wearing a blue Air Force general's tunic, with embroidered gold leaves on the collar and stars on the shoulder boards. To impress he was wearing his considerable collection of service ribbons and medals, including the Hero of the Soviet Union and the Order of the Red Star, which were pinned to his chest. Like most older Soviets, the general looked older than he actually was - in his case, the result of a combination of too much stress and vodka over the years. He was bald, with a pencil-thin moustache, his bloodshot weasel eyes framed within a deeply lined face.

He had been in the Soviet military since graduating with a PhD in Nuclear Physics from the Technical University of Kiev, in the Soviet Republic of Ukraine, in

2

1948. His whole career had been devoted to the study of nuclear missiles, both Soviet and American. The general looked towards the open door where he could see an officer accompanied by two civilians, who he already knew to be Americans.

"Good morning gentlemen. I've been looking forward to meeting you. Please come in and take a seat. Thank you, that will be all," he said to the officer standing at the open door.

"Which one of you is Mr. Williams?"

"I am," responded the taller of the two strikingly handsome men.

Gerry Williams appeared to be in his early thirties. He was lean and powerful looking, with short dark hair, brown eyes and a square jaw. He was wearing an open neck, light blue shirt under a heavy grey suit. He didn't look happy.

The general leaned over the table, shook his hand, handed him a large envelope and said, "Your personal belongings, Mr Williams. I trust you will find them in order?"

Williams tipped the contents of the envelope out onto the polished veneer table in front of him. He slipped his tiger's eye ring back onto the ring finger on his right hand, secured his watch band on his left wrist and checked the money in his treasured alligator skin wallet. He put the wallet, his keys, comb and cigarette lighter into his various pockets. Then he looked up and said, "I hope you found what you were looking for? I see you didn't return my passport."

"Mr. Williams, I know you haven't been treated very well since your arrival here in Moscow," responded the general. "Please accept my apologies but for the time being, we will be keeping your passport.

You must be Mr. Shelby," he continued, leaning over the table to shake the other man's hand.

Peter Shelby appeared to be in his mid-thirties, with short blonde hair and an ashen complexion. He looked to be in excellent shape also. He had taken off his overcoat and was wearing a navy blue crew neck sweater and matching navy pants. He looked to be somewhat unsure of his surroundings and was fixated on the general sitting in front of him.

The general passed a large envelope to him saying, "Your personal belongings, Mr Shelby."

Shelby opened the envelope, looked inside and checked the contents. He told the general that everything seemed to be there, except for his passport and placed the envelope down on the chair beside him.

"Gentlemen, please get comfortable," said the general, mainly for Shelby's sake.

The general began to talk in a low, drowsy monotone voice; his English was excellent. "Unfortunately, I have some bad news for you both. Our meeting here this morning is one of those situations where, when I have told you what I have to tell you, I will have to kill you 'unless'. You will find out what the 'unless' is by the end of our discussions. The good news is that you are the chosen ones. Do you have any idea how many Westerners visit the Soviet Union every year? Literally thousands, a significant number of them never seeing the light of day again. Anyway, I am digressing. I take it the two of you have met, if only briefly, so I will introduce myself. I am General Vladimir Tsoff of the Soviet Strategic Rocket Forces Division of the Soviet Department of Defence.

My prime responsibility for many years now has been to supply the Defence Council of the Supreme Soviet with information on the latest developments in the nuclear arsenals of both the Soviet Union and the United States. As you might know, the arms race has been extremely close over the last three decades; our two countries have been racing neck and neck to see who could gain a strategic advantage. Both nations have built up a more-than-adequate nuclear deterrent, to the point where a stalemate position has essentially been reached and de-escalation has become most desirable. The one big difference between our two countries has been that the United States has managed to support a significant number of conventional and nuclear defence programs, while at the same time sustain a relatively buoyant economy and high standard of living for its people. The Soviet Union on the other hand, although defensively debatably perhaps slightly superior, continues to face economic decline. I have been asked to look into ways to minimize spending on our nuclear arsenal, in order to use any savings to prop up the spluttering economy. My ultimate goal for a long time has been the complete elimination of nuclear weapons. As you can probably imagine, it is extremely expensive to sustain a fully operational nuclear capability. If any savings can be realized and channelled back into the economy, it could help raise the standard of living of every Soviet."

"General, I'm not sure what you're getting at," said Shelby with a sigh.

"It will soon become clear," snapped the general. "Let me tell you, much work has gone into trying to slow down and even halt the production of nuclear weapons in both countries.

You may know that Strategic Arms Limitation Talks have taken place over the last decade. They became known as SALT I and II and were thought to be a step forward in trying to halt the production of Inter-Continental Ballistic Missiles. SALT I was an agreement to essentially freeze production of new launching systems. These talks concluded when the President and General Secretary signed the treaty in Moscow, in May 1972. The SALT II agreement was signed seven years later in Vienna and was intended to further limit the production of nuclear arms. To help you better understand, as you put it Mr. Shelby, what I am getting at, I have some slides which should give you a better idea of what this is all about." The general moved to the back of the room, turned on a projector and dimmed the lights. A photo appeared showing what looked like the entrance to a military base.

"That is Minot Air Force base in North Dakota, one of the largest nuclear missile sites in the United States. It is home to six Strategic Air Command missile squadrons, with a total of three hundred ready-to-launch missiles, with a combined payload of well over one thousand nuclear warheads," the general continued, flipping to the next slide, which showed an impressive-looking rocket.

"That, gentlemen, is a Minuteman missile, capable of carrying a payload of three, one hundred kiloton nuclear warheads." He flipped to the next slide which showed another rocket. "That is the so called Peacekeeper missile, capable of carrying a much bigger payload of ten, five hundred kiloton nuclear warheads," he said, bringing up the room lights.

"As you can see, gentlemen, these are awesome and frightening weapons, capable of causing mass destruction and lasting misery. If a quote, accident, unquote, ever occurred on a base involving one of these weapons; it would create a national dilemma and cast their future into doubt. Over the years, my department has been putting proposals forward on how to cause such a quote, accident, unquote, but to date, none of them has been accepted by the Supreme Soviet. Now, with your coincidental arrival in Moscow, I think I may have a chance of getting one of my proposals approved."

The general went back to where the projector was, dimmed the room lights and clicked to another slide which seemed to be an aerial photograph which, as far as Williams and Shelby could tell, was a close-up of the dark side of the moon. He continued, "This is a computer-enhanced spy satellite photograph of the northern part of the base. To try and minimize the losses due to retaliatory missile strikes, the underground missile silos are five miles apart."

The general pointed to a barren-looking area on the photograph. "Here, below ground, is a launch control facility; there is one of these for every flight or ten silos. The unmanned missile silos, eighty feet deep, are constructed of concrete and are adjacent to a three-level maintenance room containing environmental control equipment. The missiles are actually fired from these remote underground launch control facilities, which are manned twenty-four hours a day. The health of each missile and its support systems is continually monitored. Any of the missiles can also be fired from airborne command posts during a conflict."

The general turned the room lights up, switched the projector off and walked back to where the Americans were sitting somewhat wide-eyed.

"Gentlemen, you have an opportunity to help ensure that the world will be rid of the threat of these menacing weapons before the end of the twentieth century. We must do all we can to tame the atomic demon for the benefit, rather than the destruction, of mankind."

Shelby spoke up. "Is this stuff for real, General?"

The general, looking somewhat annoyed, said with a snarl, "Mr. Shelby, I can assure you that everything I have just presented to you is factual."

Shelby asked why such a mission was still being contemplated when the Strategic Arms Limitation Talks agreements seemed to be working. The general explained that although SALT I and II were a step in the right direction, what was needed right now was to make a giant step forward to bring about rapid nuclear disarmament. Reluctantly, he told the men that the Soviet Union could not continue to keep spending as much as the United States on its nuclear defence program for very much longer in a climate of discontent and unrest in most of its Republics.

Williams chipped in, "What makes you think that one nuclear explosion in a sparsely populated region of the United States will cause the Administration and Congress to abandon their nuclear defence program?"

General Tsoff, who had calmed down somewhat, began to speak more softly. "Mr. Williams, as I am sure you are aware, in life there are no guarantees; however there is currently a public outcry over the condition of many federally-owned nuclear fuel production factories and their associated waste sites. In fact, in certain states, whole communities are beginning to link nuclear waste to unusually high rates of leukemia, Downs Syndrome and cancer-related deaths. Without a doubt, the public will be profoundly disturbed by a nuclear explosion in the heartland of their nation. Even the Canadians will be affected. This will also undoubtedly be a most unpleasant development for the new president. This could potentially result in him having to consider taking all of the nuclear missiles in the United States out of operational service."

Shelby spoke up again. "If this plan is for real, how do we know that the Soviet Union's motive is speedy disarmament and world peace, and that this is not part of a larger plan to strengthen its power in the world?"

Just as Shelby finished speaking, an officer appeared in the doorway to the meeting room.

"Let's take a break and resume again this afternoon. Please let me introduce Major Alexei Khotov; he will take you for lunch. Major, this is Mr. Williams and Mr. Shelby."

"This way gentlemen," said the major.

Before leaving the room, Shelby removed his personal belongings from the large envelope General Tsoff had given him earlier and stashed them into his various pockets. Outside the room, they saw two heavily armed guards, talking in the hallway.

Unlike the general, Major Khotov looked young, with bright eyes and a handsome face. He was wearing an immaculately cut Soviet Air Force uniform. As he led the Americans along a hallway, he asked them if they had any questions he could try and answer. His English was very good and he seemed to have more of an American accent than an eastern European one.

"You bet!" responded Shelby. He and Williams were more relaxed now that they were out of the presence of the seemingly authoritarian general. As they moved along the long dimly lit hallway, Shelby continued, "What will

I tell my friends and work associates about my extended stay in Moscow, of all places?"

"Mr. Shelby, please be assured that we will provide you with a very plausible explanation. Perhaps a prolonged illness or a serious accident of some kind," said the major.

"What about my flat in London, my job, my car and everything?"

"I emphasize that everything, no matter how trivial, will be taken care of. The things you are mentioning are minor details in the general's overall plan."

As they turned into another long hallway, Williams asked if they would be well compensated.

The major laughed. "Believe me, if you are successful, neither of you will lack for anything for the rest of your lives, if that's what you mean."

The questions continued and after traveling what seemed like miles through the maze of hallways, they came to an open area. This area was a hive of activity; some people were sitting eating and others standing in line, most wearing Soviet Air Force uniforms. There were many tables and chairs and a self-service food area. Williams and Shelby each accepted a large bowl of what looked like beef stew, helped themselves to bread rolls and were given a small carafe of what they thought was water, but later turned out to be vodka. The major also got a bowl of stew, a bread roll, and two small carafes. At the checkout, he gave the cashier a chit for all three of their meals. The major grabbed some small drinking glasses as he led Williams and Shelby to an empty table. Although initially somewhat reluctant to eat the stew, once they had their first taste, Williams and Shelby quickly ate the rest along with the bread. Neither of them quite knew what to do with the vodka.

Williams eyed the two carafes the major had and jokingly said, "How does any work get done around here in the afternoon or are you guys really immune to this stuff like they say?"

The major looked up. "You mean the vodka? Well for one thing, we need something to keep our blood warm through the long cold winters and it also makes working here a lot easier," he said laughing.

Williams had to admit he liked the major already; he had never realized how honest Soviets could be and if Major Khotov was an example, he thought he was probably going to enjoy his time here.

Although Williams and Shelby were smokers, they were taken aback by the amount of smoking that was going on in the food area. Smoke filled the air and everyone was smoking strong smelling cigarettes. The major offered them black filter tipped cigarettes from a pack featuring a woman dressed in a flowing white dress. They each took one and the major offered them a light with an impressive-looking silver lighter.

"I get these cigarettes sent to me by my parents back in the Soviet Republic of Armenia. They are called Akhtamars. I am originally from Yerevan, the capital of Armenia. It's close to the borders of Turkey and Iran. I acquired a taste for them a number of years ago," said the major.

Williams and Shelby smoked the strong Armenian cigarettes, which neither of them particularly cared for, but didn't show it. Williams commented to the major that they were certainly different from American cigarettes.

"Funny you should say that," he replied, getting the cigarette packet out of his pocket and showing it to them.

"Look, they are made by the Grand Tobacco Company and are labelled 'American Blend'."

"Are we actually in the Kremlin?" asked Shelby, unintentionally changing the subject.

"Yes. The Kremlin was originally a fortress or citadel, built on a hill at the confluence; I think you call it, of the Moskva and Neglinka rivers."

Williams said, "If you mean it is where two rivers flow together, you are correct and I am amazed you know such an English word. It's a credit to your knowledge of the language. I would venture to speculate that only one in ten thousand Americans would know the meaning of that word."

The major continued. "Within the Kremlin walls are a number of ancient cathedrals, palaces and government offices. I could give you more information if you are interested, but all you really need to know is that this is the cultural and power centre of the Soviet Union."

Williams, trying to lighten up the conversation, said, "I guess one day we can tell our grandchildren we were within the walls of the Kremlin."

After they had finished their cigarettes and vodka, the major led them back through the maze of hallways to the meeting room.

Once they were back in the meeting room, the major said, "Please get comfortable. The general has asked me to provide you with some further information about the mission."

"I guess there's no turning back for us?" enquired Williams. "Are the things the general described to us this morning top secret?"

"You are correct. There is no turning back for you and Mr. Shelby and there is only one way out, which I am sure the general will discuss with you in due course," the major replied. He turned the projector on, dimmed the lights and flipped to a slide saying, "The map you see shows the northern part of the state of North Dakota and the southern portions of the Canadian provinces of Manitoba and Saskatchewan. This is an area you will become familiar with during your training."

Pointing to the map he said, "During the mission, you will be based in this area on a farm near the Manitoba-North Dakota border. The farm is about seventy miles due north of the military base and very well situated for your purposes. You will be supported by local Soviet agents in the area. You would be surprised how many agents we have in the United States and Canada. The general's key agent in North America, Major Trsenkov, will take care of all your needs during the mission."

The major flipped to the next slide saying, "This is an approximation of the actual mission timeframe, which begins with your take-off from the farm. You will fly close to the base in an aircraft disguised as a flying saucer and one of you will parachute out from several thousand feet. The aircraft will then return to the farm. The paratrooper will enter onto the base, ski to the designated silo, set the missile warhead detonation process in motion, then ski to a nearby ski resort, where you will meet up and begin your return journey. Surrounding the actual mission, it is planned that you will fly from here to Havana, then onto Winnipeg via Montreal. Your return trip will be the exact opposite of your outbound trip. The complete mission, including travel time, is planned to be accomplished within three days."

The major flipped to the next slide. It showed a table of training activities under the headings, "Pilot and Paratrooper".

"As you can see, these are very specialized training activities. The pilot will be certified to the level required to accomplish the mission."

The major exhaled quite loudly; he wasn't used to talking this much and was definitely not immune to the vodka he had consumed at lunchtime. He could already feel a hangover coming on. He continued, "This same person will also be trained to cross-country ski. The paratrooper will be given extensive rocketry training, including the environments that the missiles are housed in. In addition, he will be trained how to trigger the nuclear detonation process and will also be trained to parachute from a low flying aircraft."

The major turned up the lights, turned the projector off and was about to ask Williams and Shelby if they had any questions, when General Tsoff entered the room saying, "Thank you, Major Khotov. I will take over from here."

The major said his good-byes and left the room.

The general told them that wherever their training took them, they were to tell no one about the mission. "People in the Soviet Union have very little and information can be turned into money," he warned. "There are people whose very existence relies on providing information to others and you would be surprised at how many foreign agents are operating in the Soviet Union. The Americans and British almost know as much about what is going on in this country as our Communist leaders.

Well, gentlemen, I am sure you must have many questions, but I would ask that you to hold them until tomorrow, when I would like you to come back to further discuss the mission."

"It's been like being back at college," Shelby muttered.

Just then, the same officer who had escorted them to the meeting room earlier in the day appeared at the open doorway.

"Please take Mr. Williams and Mr. Shelby to the KGB headquarters complex. I will see you both tomorrow," said the general as they left the meeting room.

General Tsoff followed after them, going down the hall to his dimly lit office. He slumped down into his desk chair feeling very tired. On his desk were framed photographs of his late wife and famous Soviet leaders, including Nikita Khrushchev and Leonid Brezhnev. Hanging on the wall were old paintings of Lenin and Stalin. Today had been one of the most exciting days of his career. He was pleased that he had found the Americans and felt sure they could pull off the mission; their training would confirm this. The majority of the Soviet agents in North America were unsophisticated, even though most of them were very well educated. None of them were anywhere near as worldly and well rounded as the Americans nor could they communicate anywhere near as well. In fact they were all quite rough around the edges, with very little class and none of them spoke English without an accent. Even the head of the operatives in North America was considered to be somewhat uncouth, but had proven to be very effective at carrying out orders without asking too many questions. The general didn't really trust any of his people in North America and provided them with as little information as he could to ensure that, in the event that any of them were ever apprehended, they wouldn't know anything of any consequence. They were always told what to do, without being given the big picture. This was the Soviet way. If they became too inquisitive, an unfortunate accident would be arranged - hunting accidents and poisoning were the most common methods of elimination. His superiors, the Americans, Majors Khotov and Trsenkov and himself would be the only ones who would know the full mission plan. That is how he wanted it.

He began shuffling through the folders and papers piled high on his ancient looking desk and for some reason, began to think about his late wife. She had passed away several years before after a long battle with cancer. They had never had children due to the passion he had for his work. His wife had led a very lonely life, but had been very comfortable compared to most of the other women in the Soviet Union. She could have had anything she wanted, the very best champagne and caviar if she wished, but she never took advantage of it. She spent the summers in comfortable accommodations in Yalta, directly south of Moscow on the Crimean peninsula, in the Soviet Republic of Ukraine. Located on the northern shore of the Black Sea, the area is famous for its warm dry summers and magnificent natural landscape. Surrounded by mountains with lush, Mediterranean-like vegetation growing on the lower slopes, temperatures in the months of July and August were between seventy and eighty degrees, the sea was warm and the air dry. The weeks in the summer when her husband had joined her had been the happiest of her life. He was such a passionate man, versed in the history of Alexander the Great, the Tsars and the World Wars. When he was with her, they spent their evenings walking up and down the majestic promenade along the seafront. She knew she was blessed to have such a wonderful man for a husband and respected how important his work was to him. She also accepted that he was an alcoholic. She knew that although he was involved with perhaps the most deadly weapons ever invented, he was a good man and was always full of good intentions. She knew her husband was very different in that whenever he had any spare time, he would read books and papers written by famous scientists like Einstein. Her husband had very few friends, preferring instead to work many hours a day, seven days a week, for the Soviet military. Although they hadn't seen much of each other over the years, they were really good friends in that whenever they did see each other, it was as if they had never been apart. The general had fond memories of those summer weeks he had spent with his wife. Although wholly and completely dedicated to his work, he had loved the summer sun, which always breathed new life into his aching body, but he had not been back to Yalta since his wife had died.

The general opened the bottom drawer of his desk and took out a small glass and a half-full bottle of vodka; it was time for his nightly indulgence.

\* \* \* \*

By the time Williams and Shelby got to their rooms, it was already getting dark. Williams invited Shelby into his room and checked to see if any beer or liquor had been provided. He found some in the kitchen and filled a glass with what smelled like Scotch. He dropped some ice cubes into his glass and as he came out of the kitchen, handed Shelby the beer he had asked for.

Shelby went over to the window, looked out and saw an awesome sight. The multi-colored onion shaped domes of St Basil's Cathedral and the towers along the wall of the Kremlin looked spectacular in the gathering twilight. Williams meanwhile slumped down into an armchair saying, "I think we should get to know each other, given we may be depending on each other to stay alive in the not too distant future. You start."

Shelby turned, looked over to where Williams was sitting and began. "Let me see, I'm an only child; I was married once for a short time, until my wife, or more likely her parents, decided she'd made a mistake. There were no kids in the marriage. My parents still live in North Dakota, where I am originally from. I went to college up in Minnesota and I work for an international advertising agency and have been working in their London office for just over a year. About a month ago, I came here to Moscow on a whim. I had just broken up with a lady friend and needed to get away for awhile. I was only planning on being here for two weeks. Moscow in winter really appealed to me for some strange reason. I booked a flight without much trouble and the woman at passport control at Heathrow airport checked my ticket and passport and let me through without a word. I don't think she even looked at my ticket, I guess she probably figured I was flying to the States. I arrived here and all hell broke loose. You'd have thought the Abominable Snowman had arrived. I was shuffled from one interrogation room to the next. Why had I come to the Soviet Union? Was I in the United States military? Why didn't I have a visitor's visa or entry papers of any kind? They wouldn't believe I'd just come here on two weeks vacation. I was told I would be taking the next flight out of the Soviet Bloc. That was about a month ago and I've been kept secluded in some broken-down hovel ever since. Talk about being in the wrong place at the wrong time! And now I seem to be involved in a situation where there is no way out. What do you think? Do you think there is any way out of this for us?"

"It seems to me that you and I are in too deep already, after what we were told today and did you see the number of barrel-chested, Goldfinger-look-a-likes, standing around on every floor of this building? Anyway why don't you speak to the general about it tomorrow?" Williams suggested.

"What about you?" asked Shelby.

Williams began, "About three weeks ago, I arrived here, but unlike you, I did have the appropriate papers for a visiting westerner. However, I didn't come here just to be a tourist. I was working in sales for IBM in New York City and was their number one salesman globally last year. You know, something happens to you when you become number one at something. You feel as if there is nothing left to achieve; it's weird. I'm originally from Albany, New York, had a pretty normal upbringing - a public and high school education. I spent several years at Syracuse University where I majored in Business Administration, a totally generalist degree. I played on the varsity football and hockey teams during my first and second years there, but was only a fill-in, not a first stringer on either team. My first job was in sales for a business machine company in Syracuse. After working there for several years I joined IBM. I initially worked out of a regional sales office in

Rochester and sold so well, that they moved me to their US sales headquarters in New York City.

My father was a prisoner of war in Vietnam for several years and although he was eventually released, he never recovered and is in an upstate New York mental institution. My mother was killed a few years back in an automobile accident involving a carload of drunken teenagers. My sister recently married an Aussy and moved to Australia. I've never been married. I have an apartment in lower Manhattan and can see the Staten Island Ferry going back and forth all day long. I paid the landlord two years' rent in advance to keep it for me, just in case things don't work out. With my father's condition, my mother's death and my sister's move to Australia, I figured I'd give Communism a try."

"What do you mean, give Communism a try?"

"I thought I could perhaps get a job with IBM or some other computer company in Moscow; you know, the international language of the computer business is English and I have a lot of experience in computer sales and lots of ideas on how to be successful in the computer industry," Williams replied.

"It just seemed funny when you said you would give Communism a try, especially when you were born and grew up in the States."

"I'm sure people all over the world try different things every day," said Williams. "I was looking for a new challenge, and anyway I've pretty much had it with the States and all it stands for. There's got to be something better."

Just then there was a knock on the door and Shelby, being the closest, went over and opened it. Standing in the hallway were two of the most beautiful women he had ever seen. They had blonde hair, were wearing matching white, full-length fur coats and black, backless high heeled stilettos.

"Hello. We have come to visit with you and your friend," said one of the women in a soft sexy voice. "Could we come in?"

"Someone delivering a pizza?" yelled Williams jokingly, from inside the room.

Shelby didn't hear Williams, as he had lapsed into a trance. Quickly coming out of it he said, "Yes, yes, please come in."

The women entered the room and on seeing them, Williams was taken aback, but he managed to jump up, rush over and begin the introductions.

"Well hello there! I'm Gerry and this is Peter. Would you ladies like a drink and could I take your coats?"

The woman who had previously spoken, said, "Yes, two vodkas please, no ice and we'll keep our coats on for now, thank you."

Williams went into the kitchen, found a bottle of what he thought was vodka from its smell, quickly poured two drinks, came back into the room and handed the drinks to the two absolutely gorgeous women.

"To what do we owe the pleasure of your company?" asked Williams.

The second woman spoke. "General Tsoff mentioned you might like some company tonight; he told us you gentlemen are very important and wants us to give you a good time."

"Well, wasn't that nice of old Tsoffy? Don't you think so, Pete?"

"Yes, oh yes," said Shelby coming out of another trance.

The woman who had spoken first introduced herself as Natasha and her friend as Anna and said, "Anna is from Moscow and I am from near Saint Petersburg. We are both with the Intelligence Service. Anna is an assistant to a member of the Council of Ministers and I work for several members of the Congress of People's Deputies."

Anna spoke up. "General Tsoff told us you are from America. Please tell us about it; we have seen some Hollywood movies and it seems wonderful."

"What movies have you seen?" asked Williams.

"Let me think; help me Natasha," said Anna.

Natasha said, "*Gone with the Wind* and *Breakfast at Tiffany's* are my favourites."

"Those are classic movies," replied Williams.

"You know, we still only see movies in black and white," said Natasha.

"Things have changed a lot in America since those movies were made; these days things are not as innocent as they were then," said Williams. "Some of the latest movies portray life pretty much as it is."

"What do you mean?" asked Anna.

"Well, there are now movies about how horrible war can be, how hard it can be living in a poor neighbourhood and others about crime and murder," Williams replied.

"This sounds similar to the way things are here in the Soviet Union. We thought things were different in America, but they sound like they are the same," Natasha frowned.

"We thought everyone in America drove big fast cars, had swimming pools and lots of money," said Anna.

"Some people do, but the majority of the people probably live similar lives to the average Soviet. I think you get a particular stereotype of Americans from watching old Hollywood movies," said Williams.

"Do you and Peter have a good life there?" Anna asked.

Shelby spoke up. "Actually, I've been living and working in London for the past year and it's a great city."

Williams said, "I've been dealing with a lot of personal problems lately, but anyway, let's hear about you. Can I freshen up your drinks?"

"Mine's fine, thank you."

"Mine too, thank you."

"For us there is not much to tell," Anna said. "We are just starting our careers."

"Who's staying in this room?" asked Natasha.

"That would be me little old me," responded Williams.

"Not too little I hope?" giggled Natasha.

Anna turned to Shelby and said, "Would you like to show me your room?" Before Shelby could answer, she was ushering him into the adjoining room. After watching Shelby and Anna leave, Williams turned and saw that Natasha had let her coat fall open and to his great delight, was wearing nothing but a bra, garter belt and nylons, all black. She threw her coat off and moved to where he was sitting, knelt down, unzipped his pants and quickly went to work. She was an expert with her mouth and began to make Williams curse out loud.

After a while, she suggested they find the bedroom. Williams quickly got undressed, pulled back the sheets and slid in. Natasha threw off her high heels and got in beside him. Williams removed her bra and began to kiss her red hot nipples. He felt down between her legs and began to manipulate her like a puppet, making her twitch and cry out in unison with his gentle touches. After several minutes she let out a huge sigh and pushed his hand away.

"Thank you," she said breathlessly. "Now, it's your turn."

Williams easily slipped into her as she moved on top of him and within a few never-to-be-forgotten moments, had erupted inside her.

Next door, Shelby and Anna had found the bed and she was attacking him with her mouth. Shelby had once again relapsed into a trance, thinking this couldn't really be happening. Anna found a working rhythm and quickly took him to paradise, leaving him gasping. Shelby, wanting to satisfy her, buried his head between her nylon-covered legs and busied himself with pleasuring her.

It would be a night of pure ecstasy for both men.

\* \* \* \*

The next morning when they awoke, they were alone, which didn't seem like a big deal as Natasha and Anna had said they were staying in the same complex. They rushed through their room service breakfasts and were escorted back to the meeting room where they had met the general the day before.

General Tsoff greeted them as they came through the door.

"Good morning gentlemen. I trust you slept well," he said with a wink.

"You can be assured of that!" said Williams, returning the wink.

"Please take a seat. Are you both ready to continue?"

Shelby came alive nodding and said, "General, it seems you have chosen me for this mission. Can I ask why?"

"You and Mr Williams, you are perhaps the most physically fit Americans I have encountered for quite sometime. As you probably know, most of your fellow countrymen are usually overweight and out of shape."

"That aside," said Shelby, "Don't I get a say in this?"

"I'm afraid not. You chose to come here and in the Soviet Union, people are recruited whenever they are needed, for the good of the Motherland."

"This is crazy!" said Shelby angrily. "For the good of the Motherland? I am an American, not a Soviet. I came here on vacation and I obviously wouldn't have come if I knew this was going to happen to me!"

"Would you rather spend the next twenty years as a political prisoner in Siberia? I hear Siberia has wonderful skyscapes at this time of the year. I can easily arrange this, by fabricating sufficient drug smuggling or spying evidence to convict you. You know, you should really have done your homework before coming here. Have you ever heard the famous expression, *When in Rome do as the Romans do*? Well, I think this is applicable to the situation you find yourself in at the moment - only replace Rome with Moscow and Romans with Soviets. You know, you and Mr Williams should feel honoured that you have been chosen for this mission. Anyway, you did come here and that is all that really matters at this point in time. Why don't you look on the bright side? Once the mission is completed successfully, you will be on vacation for the rest of your life."

Williams broke into the conversation. "While we are on this subject, why do you think I want to join the Soviet

Air Force? I had decided to give Communism a try, not the Soviet military."

"As I just told Mr Shelby, as soon as you arrived on Soviet soil it was our prerogative as to what to do with you. Most people we could care less about, but you and Mr Shelby are special and ideal for the mission."

"How do you know?" shouted Williams angrily. "Really, how do you know this?"

The general stood up and leaning forward over the table, shouted, "Calm down, Mr Williams!"

With the discussion suddenly becoming very loud, there was a knock at the open door, an armed guard stood at the door looking into the room and asked if everything was alright.

"Yes, everything is fine," said the general, walking over to the door, closing and locking it.

Shelby continued, "How can you do this to us? I came here on vacation. I am not a Soviet. I am not a citizen of this country. This is absolutely ridiculous!"

"I understand how you feel, Mr. Shelby, but you must understand when you come to a foreign country, you have to follow that country's rules," the general replied.

"I can understand that, but surely you cannot force someone to join the military. This is insane and you also want us to attack our own country. This situation is truly unreal," said Shelby.

"Mr. Shelby, you came to this country of your own free will. Nobody forced you to come here. You know, we could debate this for days, but the fact is, you are here and we need you to do a job for us," said the general sternly. "As I said earlier, if you want to spend the next twenty years in Siberia, this can be arranged."

"Obviously, I don't want to do that, but why do I have to do anything you want me to?" Shelby replied.

"That is the way it is, unfortunately. I'm sorry but we need your assistance and if we don't get it, your life as you know it will essentially be over."

"Well, I guess I really have no choice, but this whole thing is unbelievable. I can't believe this is really happening to me and I don't understand how you can do this to me! I really don't," said Shelby.

"I take it from what you said earlier you feel the same way Mr. Williams?"

"Well, it wasn't my intention to join the Soviet military upon my arrival here, but I do understand what you are trying to accomplish. I am willing to go on the mission, provided you keep your word about setting us up for life afterwards," Williams replied.

"You can both be assured that I will keep my word. This will be the greatest mission in the history of the Soviet Union. Keeping my word will not be a problem," said the general proudly. He handed them some papers. "If you gentlemen could sign these, I would be most grateful."

While they were signing the papers, Major Khotov entered the room.

"Gentlemen, Major Khotov will be responsible for your training over the next year and you know, of course, that the Soviet Union will be forever in your debt when you have succeeded in accelerating nuclear disarmament. Our government will ensure that you are comfortable for the rest of your lives, in the place of your choosing, anywhere in the world. This, gentleman, is all I have to tell you, except that I will now do my best to answer any questions you may have." The general sat down.

Williams asked the first question. "One thing that has been puzzling me about your plan is flying to the base in an aircraft disguised as a flying saucer. Why couldn't we just drive there?"

General Tsoff started to smile for the first time in two days, and said excitedly, "Mr. Williams, you have asked an excellent question. I must tell you, I am extremely pleased to see that you have been taking what the major and I have been presenting to you, seriously."

Williams cut in. "Alright General, can you please just answer the question?"

"Please Mr. Williams, I had not really planned on getting into such detail here today, as all aspects of the mission will be presented to you in great detail during your training. However, I see no reason why I shouldn't answer your question at this time. As I mentioned yesterday, we have been planning this mission for many years. One of the things we have discovered during that time is that the guards at the border crossings north of Minot Air Force base are trained to be very observant of unfamiliar persons crossing the border. They normally enter your vehicle license plate number into their system, and unless they already have you on file, search your vehicle, often with the help of sniffer dogs. Therefore, when one of you crosses the border to meet the other at the ski resort, although you will be driving, you will be clean and shouldn't have a problem with having your vehicle searched; all they should find is ski equipment. However, the night of the mission, if they searched your vehicle, they would find some unusual electronic equipment and firearms, as you call them. As for your question regarding disguising the aircraft as a flying saucer the night of the mission, I am sure you both know from browsing through the tabloids,

I think they're called, there are always sensational articles about people who say they saw a flying saucer somewhere in a remote part of the United States. Therefore, it is conjectured that even if you are seen by someone - an extremely remote possibility given the bleak frozen terrain you will be flying over in the dead of night - disguised as you will be, they will have the problem of deciding whether or not what they really saw was a flying saucer and who to tell, who would believe them?"

Williams asked, "Don't these bases have sophisticated radar for detecting approaching aircraft?"

"Good point Mr. Williams. Of course they do, but it is planned that you be flying so low on your approach to the base that night, that you will be lost in the ground clutter and filtered out of any screen-displayable data. Even if you do momentarily show up on radar, it will be three in the morning. All the base fighters should be grounded at that time and they will not be expecting a hostile aircraft that close to the base in the interior of the country. Their guard should be down. These are the assumptions we are making, based on our own Soviet system. I hope that answers your question?"

"Yes," said Williams looking at Shelby.

The general continued. "What do you think surveillance and espionage are all about? Obviously, one of the main purposes is to allow organizations to work out almost every angle and detail of a mission before it is undertaken, thus ensuring its success in most cases. However, even the best of planners sometimes neglect one or two minor details during the planning of every mission and that is where you and Mr. Shelby come in."

The general sighed; he looked very tired - too tired. Williams figured he must be dying of some debilitating disease; nobody could look that tired just from a lack of sleep. The general was now breathing heavier and asked if there were any more questions.

Williams asked, "What if we have problems?"

"We will do everything we can to get you back safely." Williams didn't really believe this and had a bad feeling in the pit of his stomach, but figured he could look after himself if it became necessary.

"Do you have any other questions?" asked the general.

"Yes" said Shelby. "I have one. Will Natasha and Anna be coming to visit us again tonight?"

"Mr. Shelby, unfortunately Natasha and Anna are very busy in the service of their country. They are both still undergoing training. However, I am sure before your training is over, they will visit you again. By the way, I hear they enjoyed last night as much as you and Mr. Williams probably did. When they will visit you again, I cannot say. Sorry. Any more questions?"

There was a pause and then the general spoke again, this time, more quietly. "For your information, the Supreme Soviet approved your training last night, so the mission should be approved also. Thank you both and I will see you in approximately one year from now. Oh I nearly forgot the 'unless'. The "unless" is that you fully execute the mission as planned. Now that you know what the 'unless' is, please train well so you will be able to carry out this mission successfully. Please be aware that if you don't complete the mission, we will track you down and kill you. Please have no doubt about this if opportunities to escape present themselves to you."

General Tsoff wished them well, shook their hands and Major Khotov led Williams and Shelby from the meeting room to one of the barracks within the Kremlin garrison. Their training had begun.

\*　\*　\*　\*

Unexpectedly, the first weeks of their training consisted of no training at all, but instead a series of tests and what seemed like every medical examination known to man. Although the mission was planned to last for only a few days, it seemed the general wanted them to be in excellent, if not, perfect physical condition. From the numerous tests and examinations they had undergone, it was determined that Williams was in top physical shape apart from one serious problem - a weak left knee. It seemed he had cartilage damage from an old sports injury which would need to be repaired. As a result of this surgery, he had all his classroom training during the first six months. His field training would follow, when his knee was fully rehabilitated.

Shelby's tests and examinations showed he was also in excellent physical condition, except his eyesight and hearing were not at the required levels to train as a pilot. He had corrective eye surgery and treatments to remove tiny blockages in his ears. This delayed the start of his training for several weeks, during which time he managed to improve his already considerable physique.

William's classroom training took place at the Moscow Institute of Physics and Technology, the Flight Test Centre at Balkinur and the Security Assessment and Training Centre at Sergie Prosad. By far his most intense training was on the computer systems and software within the Minuteman missile. He was amazed that the Soviets had so much detailed information about American missiles.

Although he had always been in computer sales, he knew enough about patching software that he was confident he could make the required modifications when the time came. He learned in-depth, about nuclear bomb design and the processes of nuclear fission and fusion. He was instructed why there are slow and fast neutrons, and heavy and light atoms. It seemed to Williams that nuclear bombs were all about the bombardment of atoms and isotopes by neutrons under extremely high temperatures. It was all very interesting and he was beginning to feel like the proverbial rocket scientist.

Shelby, whose main function would be to fly Williams to the base the night of the mission, spent many months at Vukovo Airfield training to be a pilot. He passed the written tests with extremely high scores and completed one hundred hours of classroom study. He took his flying lessons in a Soviet Yakolev two-seater trainer aircraft, with a top speed of two hundred kilometers an hour and a range of seven hundred. He received over ninety hours of pilot training with an experienced Soviet squadron leader and over sixty hours of solo flight training. Most of his flight training was at night, like the mission would be. By the end of his flight training, Shelby felt quite at home flying the YAK trainer and enjoyed flying so much he planned to take it up as hobby when the mission was over.

Williams's field training was concentrated on the SS series of missiles located in silos in Uzyhar and Tatchevco in the eastern Soviet Union. He learned about the various rocket stages, guidance and inertial navigation systems of Inter Continental Ballistic Missiles. He lived with the missile system operators and technicians and learned how warm and friendly Soviets could be. They worked very hard during the day and played just as hard at night. A normal day would consist of getting up early, washing in a basin of warm water, putting on several layers of clothing and having a hearty breakfast. Lunch consisted of sandwiches he had made the night before. In the evening, he would eat hot catered food with the other operators and technicians in one of the insulated shacks on the base. After the meal, he would play cards or watch TV, especially if there was a hockey or soccer game on. By the time he had completed his training, he knew about the majority of the systems required to support the various stages of a missile. He could easily find his way around the inside of a silo and knew how to gain access to the missile's electronics equipment.

In November, Williams's training switched to the Vukovo Airfield, southwest of Moscow, where Shelby was still undergoing his flight training. For a number of weeks, he learned about parachute harness packing and jumping. He made jumps from towers from heights up to four hundred and fifty feet and during the final weeks, practiced parachute jumping out of low flying aircraft. By the end of his training, he had overcome the fear of jumping and was able to hit the ground standing upright, in designated landing areas.

Towards the end of their training, Shelby and Williams trained together. Shelby flew the Yakolev flight trainer at very low altitudes and Williams practiced parachute jumping. Williams did four jumps each day, two in the morning, one in the afternoon and one at night, until they became routine.

Once they had completed their flight and parachute training, they returned to the barracks in the Kremlin garrison and began sleep-depravation training. They were trained to be able to perform complex tasks for several days at a time, without sleep. The use of energy enhancing stamina pills was a necessary part of staying alert and they got used to taking them. They learned that this is what gives agents an edge over regular people, who would eventually become tired and fall asleep. On the last day of this training, they were each given cyanide pills and told to use them if they were ever in a situation where they would rather die than live.

A few days later, they spent a day at a firing range outside Moscow, which was perhaps the most fun they had during their whole year of training. They fired off round after round from Russian AK-47 automatic assault weapons and semi-automatic Makorov P-8 pistols. They learned that the AK-47 designed and developed by Mikhail Kalashikov at the end of the Second World War, is still the most widely used weapon in the world today. Firing at targets, pinned to bales of hay, on the side of a snowy hill was really fun for them. The intent of their weapons training was to ensure they were comfortable using firearms. If they had to do any shooting, they would likely be shooting from the hip, so they didn't need to be sharpshooters or marksman. Williams remembered he'd had an air gun in his teens, which was the only gun he'd ever owned or fired. Shelby had been hunting with his father several times and had been allowed to fire his father's hunting rifle on occasion. He thought it was either a Remington or Winchester. He had never owned a gun himself. Neither of them had certainly ever fired multiple round rapid fire assault weapons before. After the day at the firing range, they both had sore shoulders from firing off so many rounds. The day at the firing range had come just before they were due to leave for their cross-country skiing training.

Their ski training took place in Murmansk, near the Arctic Circle. Every year the Festival of the North, a mini Winter Olympics, is held there. Their cover story was that they had won a trip-of-a-lifetime contest and because they had heard of the Murmansk Festival of the North, thought they would like to experience it for themselves.

William's training was far more intensive than Shelby's because of the skiing he would be doing on the base. For two weeks, he was pushed to the point of exhaustion, skiing for many hours at a time, with different instructors, at different times during the day.

While they were at Murmansk, Williams and Shelby met the local Karelians and people from all over northern Scandinavia. They found out that most of them had never heard of America. They had both learned a number of Russian words during their training, but still had trouble putting sentences together. They had learned greetings, small talk and many other expressions used in daily life. When talking to people it was nice to be able to speak their language, if only just a little bit, especially when very few of them spoke any English.

The days spent skiing and the nights spent socializing were most welcome after the previous year of intense studying and training. The weeks they spent in Murmansk were most memorable and a wonderful finale to their year of training before they had to make the long train ride south, back to Moscow, where they were scheduled to meet with General Tsoff the next day.

*   *   *   *

Leading up to the meeting with the Americans, as he had begun to call them, General Tsoff had attended a number of high level meetings with the Chairman of the Supreme Soviet. Although the chairman had approved the training for the Americans the year before, he had still not given approval for the mission to go ahead. The general had made a number of detailed presentations and had returned to answer questions on several occasions. He had also prepared a number of mission briefs. The chairman was concerned that Williams would not have the sufficient knowledge and experience to set the warhead detonation process in motion. General Tsoff was concerned that the chairman might not approve the mission because if it went wrong, it may lead to a nuclear confrontation between the superpowers. However, after reviewing the impressive training reports of the Americans and being aware of the thorough planning done by the general, the chairman had given his approval for the mission to proceed. He knew that for the Communist Party to survive, they had to start improving the lives of each and every Soviet. The mission seemed like a perfect vehicle to help bring a speedy end to the nuclear arms race and launch a more prosperous era for the Soviet Union.

Williams and Shelby looked well tanned as they entered the familiar meeting room; the general had thought of everything. They would both be expected to have good tans after a week in Cuba. Pale complexions on such good looking men would most certainly draw attention to them. In front of them were brand new uniforms, large envelopes and small, velvet-covered cases. The general had just presented these to them in an impromptu ceremony.

Williams had been given a Soviet Paratrooper uniform, badges for completing rocketry and parachute training and a master skier certificate. Shelby had been given a Soviet Air Force uniform, pilot's wings and an expert skier certificate. They had also been presented with plaques displaying the Soviet Strategic Rocket Forces Division of the Soviet Department of Defense insignia.

General Tsoff congratulated them both once more, wished them luck and asked an officer to escort them over to the KGB headquarters complex, a place with which they were also very familiar.

*    *    *    *

Back in his office, General Tsoff was in a thoughtful mood that night. Although he knew for sure that Williams had the right stuff, he still wasn't sure about Shelby; he seemed like too much of a dreamer. That is why he had given him the lesser mission responsibilities. He knew it wasn't going to be easy and potentially a multitude of things could go wrong. He chuckled to himself that even in the Soviet Union they were familiar with Murphy's Law.

The general remembered a famous proverb "Everything comes to he who waits" and this was one of the happiest nights of his life. He knew the Soviet Union was taking a huge gamble undertaking this mission, because if the Americans got caught, the incident could lead to World War III.

He opened the bottom drawer of his desk and took out a small glass and an unopened bottle of vodka.

On the way over to the KGB headquarters complex, Williams wondered if the women would visit them that night. Unbeknownst to Shelby, Williams had been with several women during his year of training. He had romanced a young nurse while he was rehabilitating his knee and had been with a technician's sister while training at the Uzyhar missile base. In return, he had told the technician he would do whatever he could to get him and his family to the States when his secret mission was over. He'd also had a one-night stand with a waitress at the resort where they had just been staying in Murmansk. He guessed Shelby hadn't had sex since the last time the women had visited them, but he didn't know for sure and wasn't going to ask.

As they entered William's room, they found Natasha and Anna sitting on the couch clad in skimpy see-through negligees, both looking amazingly sexy. They were both holding glasses, which, if William's memory served him well, would have vodka, no ice in them.

"Wow!" said Williams. "Our prayers have been answered once again, Pete."

Shelby had gone into a predictable trance, fixated on the women.

"Hey Pete, what's your poison?" asked Williams, making his way towards the kitchen.

Shelby came out of his daze and asked for a beer.

Williams grabbed two beers and handed one to Shelby as he came out of the kitchen. "Well ladies," he said, "I'm sure I don't need to tell you how wonderful it is to see you again."
He moved over to the couch and clinked the women's glasses. "Na Zdorovje!"

"Na Zdorovje," said Natasha and Anna, laughing.

Natasha said, "I hope you don't mind, but we asked a cleaner to let us in."

"I certainly don't mind; how about you Pete?" said Williams as he was moving around to the back couch. He leaned forward and put his arms around Natasha and Anna.

"I wish I had a camera; this is definitely one of life's special moments," he laughed, hugging both women around the neck.

Williams and Shelby alternately told the women about Murmansk and the Festival of the North. Natasha and Anna seemed to be most impressed and while Shelby was still talking, Williams got up and went over to the window overlooking Red Square. He was thinking that although he had been in the Soviet Union for over a year now, he had still not seen any of the sights of Moscow. Natasha noticed him looking out of the window and got up and went over to where he was standing.

"You seem to be in deep thought. What are you thinking about?" she asked.

"Oh, just what a wonderful old city this seems to be and so far I haven't seen any of it."

"I'll tell you what. If I'm allowed, when you get back, I'll personally show you around; how about that?" she said, pecking him on the cheek.

Williams, smiling, said, "You have a deal; that would be wonderful."

Anna shouted to them to come and join her and Shelby, to discuss the plans for the night.

"This sounds exciting," said Williams, coming back over towards the couch with Natasha.

Anna told them that they wanted to swap partners - she with Williams and Natasha with Shelby.

"That is, if you don't mind of course?" she said.

39

"Sounds good to me," said Williams. "What do think Pete? Any problem with you?"

"No" said Shelby, shaking his head in agreement, transfixed on the women once again.

Natasha took Shelby's hand and led him towards the adjoining room. He was emotionally overcome with Natasha's attractiveness and began to sigh as she embraced and kissed him. Her perfume was overpowering and her nipples were hard and hot. She quickly undressed him, removed her negligee and began to use her mouth to calm him. Shelby had never felt so good in his whole life. Natasha slowly and rhythmically took him to every man's nirvana, after which he returned the favour. They slept for awhile and worked to find their heaven on earth on several more occasions.

In the other room, Williams and Anna were entwined, finding their own paradise. Like Natasha and Shelby, they slept occasionally, but primarily pleasured each other all night.

# CHAPTER 2

*Friday February 12, 1982*

Williams and Shelby awoke alone, early Friday morning, to
the sound of Major Khotov shouting loudly and knocking
on the doors to their rooms. It was just after four thirty
and although they were very tired, they showered with
knowing smiles on their faces.

By five fifteen they were on their way to Sherymetevo
airport which they were told had been especially built for
the 1980 Summer Olympic Games. It was snowing lightly
as they entered the modern looking terminal building.
Their seats had been pre-selected, so they went directly to
the departure gate. The major spoke to a woman at the
gate, who in turn spoke to someone on the phone and they
were let through to board the aircraft. They were greeted
at the aircraft door by the aircrew and an attractive flight
attendant who took their bags and showed them to their
seats. Shelby took the window, Williams the middle and

the major the aisle seat. The seat covers showed they were flying Aeroflot Russian Airlines. Williams and Shelby had flown on a number of different airlines over the last several years, but had never had so much room or felt so comfortable. The plane was massive; however, they soon realized this might be the only highlight of the flight. There didn't seem to be any in-flight entertainment and from what they could smell coming from one of the serving areas, the food would probably not be to their liking. None of this would matter soon, as the major would be sedating both of them. General Tsoff knew that neither of the men would have had much sleep the previous night, and wouldn't get much once the mission began, so he had asked Major Khotov to ensure they slept through the flight. The major was really looking forward to his weekend in Havana; this was his first trip outside the Soviet Union and he was most excited. He envisaged himself drinking endless chilled bottles of vodka while sunbathing by the hotel pool.

After the aircraft had been de-iced, it taxied out onto the dark runway. Through the window, Shelby could see flashing lights all around. As the Russian Ilyushin aircraft took off and gained height, he could see many more lights spread out across the city, which disappeared as the aircraft ascended into dark billowing snow clouds. The major medicated them once the aircraft had reached its cruising altitude and took a stamina pill to ensure he would stay alert throughout the flight. The flight attendants had obviously been told that the major was someone special and were constantly asking him if they could get him anything. Although on duty, he had several glasses of champagne, quite a few vodkas and a number of liqueurs with unpronounceable Russian names. The flight attendants, not knowing the major's companions were sedated, were amazed at how soundly they were sleeping and were unable to offer them any food or drinks throughout the whole flight. This agitated them, even though the major kept telling them not to worry about it. The major asked the flight attendants about Havana and in a quiet moment, the most attractive one whispered that she would love to show him around when they got there. Although rather reluctant, he accepted a slip of paper from her with a phone number on it. He was thinking he should be able to get away for a few hours, even though he knew the general would be expecting him to be available at all times of the day and night. He thought he could go back to the hotel and periodically check for messages. Anyway, he would have to play it by ear.

The medication had worked perfectly and Williams and Shelby started to come awake as the huge airliner was into its final approach and golden beaches were coming into view. The airliner was approaching from over the Caribbean Sea, due to an imposed no-fly zone along the northern coast of Cuba and the Straits of Florida. As the airliner approached the airport landing strip, the shadow of the giant mechanical bird swept across the island's sparsely populated landscape. The massive passenger jet glided in over the tops of the palm trees, skirting the runway of Havana's Jose Marti International airport.

It was ten fifteen local time and Gerry Williams and Peter Shelby had arrived back in North America.

\*   \*   \*   \*

Back in Moscow, another cold winter night had set in and General Tsoff was sitting in his office, anxiously awaiting the news that Major Khotov and the Americans had arrived in communist Cuba.

Earlier in the day, he had phoned Major Trsenkov at the farm to make sure everything was ready for the Americans' arrival. The major reported that all the modifications to the mission aircraft had been made and a Ford Bronco had been hired for the Americans to use on the trip to and from the ski resort. The major asked the general if there was anything he should know about the Americans before they arrived later that evening.

"Not really," said General Tsoff, "but you should know that I need you to do everything you can to ensure the mission is successful. Please understand that this is the culmination of my career and if everything goes as planned, I will be retiring a happy man."

"I will certainly do my best. You can count on that," said Major Trsenkov. "I think you would agree, I have never let you down before."

"That is very true. Please call me as soon as the Americans have taken off from the farm. Thank you." The general hung up.

\*   \*   \*   \*

The monster aircraft came to a stop and a short time later, its front and rear doors were opened. Williams was thinking about the temperature swing; it must have been at least twenty below when they left Moscow and now they were in eighty degree heat. The sunshine and heat felt very good and he was sorry that they would be soon making their way back to the northern hemisphere. After bypassing Cuban Immigration and Customs with the major, the men met up with a heavy-set agent who handed them boarding passes. They changed in one of the airport washrooms, putting on colourful summer clothes and stashing their cold weather clothes for later use. They said goodbye to the major, who wished them luck and said he had to go and find a phone to call General Tsoff and they headed off to their departure gate. They noticed the burly agent was trailing behind them and when they got to their gate and found somewhere to sit, he sat several rows behind them. They blended in really well with the other tanned and casually dressed vacationers flying to Montreal. The Air Canada flight was on schedule and due to depart in fifty minutes. Two agents using their names had flown down from Montreal a week earlier.

Cuba had proven to be a most useful base for the Soviets since the revolution. For over two decades, they had moved agents through Cuba to all parts of North and South America. Senior members of the Communist Party had been vacationing with their families in Cuba since the early '70's.

Their plane left the ramp on time and early into the flight, Williams and Shelby noticed that everyone on board, almost without exception, was speaking French. They spoke very infrequently and pretended to be sleeping, which wasn't easy, given they had been asleep for the last nine hours. They were extremely hungry and were glad to eat the complimentary meal offered to them. Upon arrival at Montreal's Dorval airport, just under three and a half hours later, they came through Canadian Immigration and Customs without incident, using their false Canadian passports. They were asked where they were coming from and how long they had been away. Even though they looked nothing like the two Soviet agents who had flown down to Cuba the previous week, the only thing that mattered was that the names and passport numbers were the same. They were met by a nondescript agent who gave them boarding passes and showed them where to get their connecting flight. They found a washroom and changed into their cold weather clothes, packing away the summer clothes for use on the return trip. It was now four-thirty in the afternoon and their flight to Winnipeg was scheduled to leave at six. They waited at the departure gate for about an hour before boarding the plane. They noticed that the agent, who had given them their boarding passes, was standing across from their gate, reading a newspaper while they were waiting to board the aircraft.

Upon arrival at Winnipeg International airport, Williams and Shelby did not have to go through Canadian Immigration and Customs, as it was a domestic flight. In the arrivals area they were met by Major Yuri Trsenkov, a greying, grizzled-looking Russian, old enough to be their father. He was wearing a long black coat and ankle length black boots. There was a younger man with him, whom the major introduced as Sam. Sam took their bags and led the way to the exit.

The major began to make small talk with a heavy eastern European accent. "How was your trip?" he asked.

"So far, so good," said Williams.

"Well the first part of your journey is almost over. It shouldn't take us long to get to where we're going."

After putting their bags in the trunk, Sam got behind the wheel of the new-smelling, dark Lincoln. The Americans got in the back and the major got in the front next to Sam.

"I've heard a lot about you both during the last year. It sounds like you've been very well trained and are ready for the mission," said the major.

"Never been readier," responded Williams.

"That's good. We'll soon have you on your way."

The major told them he had an apartment overlooking Lake Ontario in Toronto and they said they knew where that was.

"Sounds nice," said Shelby.

"You know, I get lonely sometimes, but I enjoy living in Canada, because it has many of the same sports as the Soviet Union; ice hockey, skiing, soccer and I have even learned to enjoy American football."

Williams said, "Actually, it's Canadian Football, not American. They have three downs and we have four."

"Yes, I know that," said the major. "Toronto also has a baseball team called the Blue Jays."

"The Minnesota Twins used to be my team." said Shelby.

Following Shelby's statement, the major didn't speak again until just before they got to the farm, just over an hour later. He and Sam listened to classical music all the way. Shelby dozed off and Williams sat thinking about what he was about to do. The gravity of the situation was beginning to sink in now that it was almost time to carry out the mission.

As they approached the farm, the major told them that it was representative of those built in the Canadian prairies after the First World War and had been a grain producing farm for many years. He told them that where the farm was located, it was almost inaccessible and several dirt roads had to be navigated to get to it. He said it had been rented from an old retired Russian who had jumped at the offer of a generous monthly income for several months, and it had only been occupied for the last few weeks, since a used turbo fan Cessna had been acquired. The light aircraft had been dismantled in California and transported to the farm. Once reassembled, the major had recruited a local metal worker to fabricate the additions, telling him they were needed for a movie shoot. Four larger-than-normal lights had been attached to either side of the aircraft, creating the typical flying saucer lighted porthole effect. Test flights had shown that the new additions had not affected the aircraft's aerodynamic characteristics or performance in any way.

When Williams and Shelby entered the farmhouse, although it looked primitive, they could see people watching TV, so knew it had electricity. The major told them each agent brought groceries with them and by making use of a large freezer in one of the barns; they had accumulated a more than ample supply of food for their stay. The major told them to follow him and he took them upstairs to a small bedroom. He told them they could leave their belongings in the bedroom during their stay.

"Now, you must be hungry. How about some goulash? There are always a few pots of goulash cooking on the stove."

"That would be great," said Shelby.

"I agree," said Williams. "Airline food is not very filling."

They were both given a bowl of goulash and some fresh bread rolls. While they were eating, the major introduced them to Anton, whom the major said would be going over the flight plan with them and would be showing them the aircraft. Anton shook hands with them and left. The major told them to come and join him and Anton in the dining room when they had finished eating.

When they got to the dining room, the men found it to be a hive of activity, with many agents talking on phones. The major explained to them that the phones they were using had coders/decoders attached to them and similar coders/decoders were being used by General Tsoff and his staff in Moscow. It seemed to Williams and Shelby that the Soviet agents at the farm had formed a brotherhood of sorts, sleeping, eating and working together. Anton drew their attention to a large map laid out on the dining room table. He showed them where the farm was on the map and where they would be flying to. He told them although it would be dark, they should still be able to see rivers and roads because they would be flying so low to the ground. After spending half an hour or so with Anton, the major told them to go and relax for awhile and they went into the room with the TV and watched the local late night news for awhile.

# CHAPTER 3

## Saturday February 13

Williams and Shelby were relaxing, watching TV, when the major came into the room and said it was time for them to get ready. They went up to the small bedroom and changed into their thermal underwear and new Soviet Air Force and Paratrooper uniforms.

The major said, "You have to wear the uniforms just in case you are captured. You have to be treated in accordance with the Geneva Convention – Rules for the Treatment of Prisoners of War, which you may have heard of?"

"Yes I've heard of it," said Williams. "I always wondered what it was."

The major said, "I am not an expert on it, but my understanding of it is, if you are captured, you must be treated humanely. Some countries adhere to it; others don't. The Americans do."

"Well, things will really have gone wrong if we have to worry about the Geneva Convention," said Williams jokingly.

They were led out to a large barn behind the farmhouse. Inside was a bizarre looking plane, which they were told looked like a flying saucer when being flown at night. Anton told them that the aircraft only had enough fuel to get to the drop-off point and return to the farm. Williams thought to himself, *these people have thought of everything.* Anton showed Shelby the aircraft's cockpit controls and instrument panel, while Williams was checking the parachutes and maneuvering a large supply package closer to the side door. Once Anton was confident Shelby was sufficiently familiar with the controls, he went through the flight plan with him once more and helped him enter some waypoints into the navigation system. Satisfied that Shelby was ready, he exited the aircraft. He removed the chocks from under the aircraft's wheels and signaled to Shelby he was clear to proceed.

Shelby eased the aircraft out of the barn, towards the dimly lit, snow-covered runway. There were four or five large drums with flames rising out of them on both sides of the makeshift runway. Shelby told Williams to strap himself in and the aircraft gradually began to accelerate, creating an ever-increasing bumping sensation as it gained speed, before it became airborne. Once the aircraft had gained sufficient altitude, Shelby banked it in a westerly direction, flying west until he came to a river, which he began to follow in a southerly direction.

\*   \*   \*   \*

Back at the farmhouse, the major rang through to Moscow and informed General Tsoff that the Americans had just taken off. The general thanked him for the information and told him to keep him updated as the mission progressed. The major said he would and hung up.

\*   \*   \*   \*

Williams leaned into the cockpit and asked Shelby if he realized this was the first time that someone wasn't watching them since they had arrived in Moscow, over a year ago. Shelby said it was a good feeling.

Once he began to see the outline of the air base, Shelby flew east to the northern perimeter. He maintained as low an altitude as he could, in the hope the base radar would not detect the aircraft. He circled over the northern perimeter fence a number of times to get into the right position for the drop. Once he got positioned where he needed to be, he pulled the plane up into a steep climb, reached the required altitude and leveled off. He waved wildly and shouted to Williams to jump. Williams threw the supply package out of the side door and followed after it. Both chutes opened almost immediately and several minutes later, Williams was standing on the snow-covered, frozen ground. His landing had been precise.

He unfastened the chute's harness, broke free from the parachute and set off to find the supply package. He moved quickly, shining a high powered flashlight up into the trees and within several minutes had located the supply package. With some climbing and tugging, he managed to pull it down. He opened it up and removed the AK-47, a pistol, a sheaved hunting knife, ski equipment, metal cutters, a small axe, electronic devices, cables, garbage bags, work boots, a folded metal frame, some tools, a medical kit and a backpack. The backpack contained twenty thousand dollars and other needed supplies. General Tsoff had figured this amount of money might be of great benefit if the Americans found themselves in a tight spot during the mission but was expecting to get most of it back. The mission would be the crowning point of his career and he wanted to do all he could to make sure it was successful. The amount of money requested had been questioned by the Chairman of the Supreme Soviet, but he had approved it after the general had reasoned with him late one night. The general had told him how crucial it was to do everything possible to ensure the success of the mission, arguing that if it was successful, it could change the nuclear landscape forever.

Williams was not planning to take the medical kit with him; it had been included on a just-in-case-it-might-be-needed basis. He carefully put the electronic devices, work boots and other items into the backpack. He holstered the pistol and strapped the sheaved hunting knife to his leg. He put on his ski equipment, shouldered the automatic weapon and set off across a small clearing.

Unbeknownst to Wolford Byford, who was hiding behind some snow-covered bushes, Williams had seen him while unpacking the supply package. Williams approached the bushes Wolf was hiding behind and administered an almighty blow to the side of his head with the butt of his automatic weapon. The blow stunned Wolf and he fell sideways, lying motionless in the snow. Williams pulled his head up by the hair and wondered what the hell he was doing out here in the middle of nowhere, on a freezing cold night. Williams figured that whoever found him would figure he'd stayed out in the cold too long.

Williams headed for a gap in the trees. Within a short time, he'd reached the base perimeter fence on the opposite side of a snow-covered road. Just along from where he was standing there was a large sign, warning that this was a restricted area patrolled by armed guards and vicious sentry dogs. *Funny*, thought Williams, *the general had neglected to mention this.* He cut a hole in the fence, squeezed through and started to ski across the snowy surface of the base. He thought it was no wonder they had selected this place for a missile base; it wasn't good for much else. He knew from spy satellite photos that there should be a silo several miles south of where he was, and as he skied towards it, he periodically checked a small compass to make sure he was maintaining a southerly course.

As he skied towards the silo, red shards of light began to pierce the dark sky above the eastern horizon. As the daylight broke through, Williams couldn't see a cloud in the sky. He was now being blinded by a combination of the sun and snow and put on his anti-glare sunglasses. If it were not for the compass he had been given by Major Trsenkov, he would have been completely lost and have no idea which direction to go in. He also began to understand how important the stamina and endurance cross-country ski training that he had done was. Without it, he knew he likely wouldn't have even made it this far and he still had to ski back to the ski lodge when he was finished, a few hours from now. The biggest problem he had was the uneven terrain he was skiing over, which resulted in him having to exert a great deal of energy to even make reasonable progress. There were no groomed trails out here and because of the uneven surface, he had to put a lot of concentration into his skiing and had very little time to think about anything else, including what he was about to do once he got into the silo. He was struck by the vastness of where he found himself and knew that if it wasn't for the fact his clothes, skis and poles were all white, he could easily have been seen from the air. The wind had got up and blowing snow was often obscuring his view. It wasn't until it temporarily subsided that he saw what he knew to be a silo security fence up ahead. Finding this meant he'd found the silo.

When he reached the silo security fence and had stopped skiing, he started to feel very cold. As he struggled to get through the fence, he started to shiver and couldn't stop his teeth from chattering. He knew the silo security fence was actually a seismic shock sensor fence, designed to detect intrusion attempts by either climbing, lifting or cutting. He unfolded and carefully attached the specially-made metal frame he had brought with him, to the fence, ensuring it would maintain its structure, and cut out the fencing inside the frame. He climbed through, confident he wouldn't set off any alarms. He was now close to the silo which, from above, looked like a collection of different sized circular covers. He could see a van parked next to the main silo cover. He swapped his ski shoes for his work boots and stowed them along with the rest of his ski equipment and automatic weapon, into an orange garbage bag, which he buried in the snow. He walked towards the silo and located the concrete stairs that led down to the door leading inside. The door was closed, but unlocked, so he cautiously entered, hoping no one would be on the other side to greet him. Once inside, he could hear voices and crouched down behind a row of storage lockers.

The maintenance crew inside the silo had no idea they had a visitor early on that Saturday morning. They were busy checking the feed pipes attached to the rocket for signs of rodents. So far they had found no damage, even though a fuel line sensor had indicated there was a problem of some kind. They had replaced the faulty sensor and were standing admiring the sleek white projectile, the Stars and Stripes shining brightly in the silo lights. The seemingly awesome power of such a weapon always overwhelmed them and they hoped it would never be launched.

While he was waiting, Williams tried to thaw out his frozen fingers and thought about how his thinking was fully aligned with the general's, in that such an incident on American soil might force the people to rise up and demand an end to nuclear weapons. He was determined to make a difference and bring about change for the better. How ingenious the general's plan was, to make the missile blow itself up.

Once the maintenance crew had finished their checks, they made their way up to the top of the silo and stowed their equipment in one of the storage lockers. Williams heard them talking about going for breakfast and a few moments later, all the lights in the silo went out. He wondered why there was no emergency lighting, but never gave it another thought. He hadn't moved for quite awhile and upon hearing the silo maintenance door being slammed shut, stood up and stretched his legs.

He found his way to the light switches and turned the silo lights back on. The first thing he had to do was bypass the alarm panel, because what he would be doing soon would set off alarms. He carefully removed the duplicate alarm panel from his backpack and installed it next to the existing one. He removed the external connector cover from the existing alarm panel and connected the wires to the signal override generator in the duplicate alarm panel, doubling up the wires in each slot. Once the last wire had been inserted, he powered up the duplicate alarm panel and cut the power to the existing panel.

He made his way down a ladder onto the metal platform surrounding the upper rocket stage of the missile, allowing him to access the nosecone electronics maintenance panel. He searched around in his backpack and found the special screwdriver he had brought with him. Looking at the screwdriver in his hand, he thought to himself, *This is it! Show time - the moment of truth.*

Williams moved close to the nosecone electronics maintenance panel and attempted to remove the screws. His hand was shaking so wildly that he couldn't get the screwdriver locked on any of the screw heads. Sweat began to stream down from his brow, onto his hands, and made them wet and sticky. Until now he hadn't realized how difficult this was going to be; obviously the magnitude of what he was about to do was already overwhelming him. He began to shake uncontrollably and feel nauseous; his legs suddenly gave way and he found himself kneeling on the metal platform. *My god!* he thought, *what is wrong with me?* He had never felt so much anxiety in his life and figured he must be having some kind of panic attack. The only other times he could remember having such feelings of nervousness was before an important exam or presentation, but it had been nowhere near as bad as this. He figured his nervous system must have gone into what is called adrenaline overload, he had many of the classic symptoms of fear. Kneeling on the metal platform, he began to take in his surroundings, reached out and touched the surface of the missile, which felt steely cold. Where he had touched it, he had left a wet fingerprint. Gradually, the multiple symptoms of fear began to subside. He'd stopped sweating and his hands had stopped shaking. Feeling better and more in control, he stood up and reached up to the nosecone electronics maintenance panel again.

Not shaking as much anymore, he managed to remove the screws and had just lifted the panel away from the nosecone, when he heard voices above him. His first reaction was the maintenance crew must have returned. He heard someone saying something about the lights and heard a storage locker being opened. He thought to himself they must have been surprised to find the lights on. He hoped they wouldn't notice the duplicate alarm panel on the far wall. He carefully put the nosecone electronics maintenance panel back in place and fortuitously, it stayed there, without requiring any screws. He quietly put the screwdriver and screws into his backpack and moved out of sight behind the missile. He could hear his heart pounding as he sat there and for some reason felt completely detached from his surroundings. Several minutes later, he was brought back to reality when the silo lights went out, leaving him in total darkness. Upon hearing the silo door being slammed shut, he thought to himself that they must have returned because they had forgotten something. Now he needed to find his way up to the light switches, on the level above, in total darkness. There was not a single solitary beam of light visible anywhere in the silo, which he thought was a credit to those who had built it. He guessed everything would have been built to military specification, which he had heard of, but had never really understood what it meant until now. He was beginning to sweat again and was experiencing a choking sensation in his throat. Despite this, he stood up and felt his way around the missile. He had a rough idea where the ladder should be and started to feel his way around on the metal platform as if he was blindfolded. His heart was pounding again and he felt light headed, which was affecting his balance. He found his way to the bottom of the ladder, climbed up and once up on the next level, felt his way around again, until he found the first row of storage lockers. He knew that the light switches were off to the side of these and with both arms outstretched in front of him, walked towards where he thought they should be. He touched concrete, thinking it was the wall, but when he got closer, found it was a support pillar. He moved around the pillar until he came to the wall, then felt his way along until he located the light switches. He was just about to switch the lights on again, when he had the thought, perhaps they were being monitored and that was the reason the maintenance crew had returned. There were four light switches in total, so he tried each one until he found the lights that lit up the area where he was working and just left those lights on, hoping all the lights had to be on before any kind of an alarm signal would be sent. Anyway, he needed light, so there wasn't much he could do about it. He just hoped the maintenance crew didn't return again.

He ran his fingers through his now soaking wet hair and wiped the beads of sweat from his brow. He had begun to shake again, as he climbed down the ladder to the metal platform. He couldn't believe how this was affecting him! He dragged his backpack from where he'd hidden it behind the missile, and shakily reached up and removed the nosecone electronics maintenance panel again, revealing a large electronics rack and a tangle of cables and wires. Mimicking Strategic Air Command's top secret communications protocol, he would be making the required modifications to arm the missile's warheads and start a prolonged detonation countdown, allowing him and Shelby sufficient time to be back in Moscow before the explosion.

The return of the maintenance crew was all Williams hadn't needed, and he found he couldn't stop shaking once again. Very shakily, he took an odd looking electronics device out of his backpack, connected it to one of the back plane connectors on the electronics rack and powered it up. Just as he was about to enter the command string to start the downloading process, he paused, thinking that he really hoped positive things would come as a result of this. Not second guessing himself for long, he entered the command string to start the downloading process and after a few seconds was prompted to insert the cassette containing the new software. Once he had inserted it, he hit the small Enter key. A tiny yellow light on the top of the electronics device was supposed to start flashing, but it didn't. Williams couldn't believe it wasn't working! He'd performed the same downloading process numerous times during his training and it had worked every single time. Why wasn't it working? He thought perhaps Strategic Air Command, commonly known as SAC had changed the downloading process and the Soviets' information was out of date. Perhaps a password was needed after all, although he had been instructed it wasn't if you were directly connected to the missile's electronics rack and he had not been asked for one.

Puzzled, he ejected the cassette and inspected it. There didn't look to be anything wrong with it. He turned the wheels and the tape rolled and seemed to be working as it should. He re-inserted the cassette and tried the command string again - still nothing. Streams of sweat started to pour from his brow once again. He thought to himself that perhaps this whole thing was too much for him; after all, up until a year ago he had been a computer salesman. He hadn't been trained for years like special assignment specialists normally were. He was essentially just a regular guy. No wonder he was having problems with this! He was quickly brought back to reality when the lights started flashing on and off. He climbed back up the ladder and reset the light switch. He remembered he had once worked in an office where the lights did this at night and on weekends, to indicate to anyone working that they would be automatically turning themselves off soon. This made him a feel a bit better, knowing that the lights probably weren't being monitored. It meant it was most unlikely the maintenance crew would be returning. He made his way back down onto the metal platform and began to focus on the problem again. He had no way of diagnosing what the problem was because he had only been trained to enter the command string and observe the tiny yellow light flashing. He was racking his brain as to what could be wrong. Perhaps the programming device had been damaged during the parachute drop. The cassette seemed to be functioning correctly and had started turning slowly once he'd pressed the Enter key. He was still sweating and shaking but was beginning to feel in control again. He began to focus on the cable with the large connector on the end. He disconnected it from the missile's electronics rack and looked at the connector and it looked fine. He looked as best he could at the pins in the connecting slot in the missile's electronics rack and they looked straight and undamaged. He powered the electronics device down, reconnected the cable, turned the power on and within a few seconds, the command prompt appeared on the small display screen. Shakily he entered the download command string again. The cassette started to turn slowly and the tiny yellow light began to flash. It was working! Williams jumped up, shot his fist into the air and shouted, "Yes!"

The only difference between this time and last time was that the cassette was already loaded in the electronics device when he entered the initial command string. He thought back to his training and remembered the cassette had always been inserted into the device. Not having the cassette already loaded seemed to have been the problem. Even though you were prompted to insert the cassette, if it wasn't already loaded, there must be some kind of software bug. When the tiny yellow light stopped flashing, a tiny green one came on, which meant the software had been successfully downloaded. He entered a command to activate the newly downloaded software and the green light turned off which indicated the new software was being executed. He had done it! From what he knew the detonation countdown should now be underway. It had taken him an hour and a half to successfully download the new software. Now that it was done, he disconnected the electronics device and cable and using a pair of pliers, pulled the majority of the pins off all the electronics rack back plan connector slots, rendering them unusable. He screwed the nosecone electronics maintenance panel back on so that outwardly there was no sign it had been tampered with.

He still had another task to take care of before leaving the silo. He had to damage the main silo cover controls sufficiently to ensure the missile couldn't be launched or extracted. He took the small axe out of his backpack, climbed up to the hydraulic control box above the missile and vigorously smashed at it several times. He broke the cover and badly damaged most of the servo motors and cogs inside. The damage was extensive. *Good job!* he thought; it will take them a while to fix this baby.

\*    \*    \*    \*

Wolf awoke to bright sunshine and found himself lying in the snow on top of a shrub with yellow flowers. He felt colder than he could ever remember and it hurt him to move his fingers, even slightly. He hoped they weren't frostbitten. He noticed frozen blood on the shoulder of his jacket and although he felt dizzy, could clearly recall what had happened only a few hours earlier. He remembered seeing the flying saucer, the parachutes and the paratrooper, who had jumped him. All he could think about right now was getting warm. He struggled to his feet and picked up his hunting rifle. He hooked the strap over his shoulder, and painfully began to make his way towards the road. Every bone in his body ached with every step he took; his toes and fingers were throbbing. As he slowly made his way through the snow-covered trees, he couldn't help thinking that he had been witness to something very sinister. The paratrooper, who had left him for dead, was obviously a professional.

Wolf's sense of direction was excellent and he came out of the woods close to where his truck was parked. With great difficulty he managed to remove the keys from his jacket pocket and unlock the driver's side door. He threw the hunting rifle onto the passenger seat and pulled himself up onto the driver's seat.

Wolf managed to start the engine and as he was reaching to turn the heater fan to maximum, noticed it was fifteen minutes past eleven. Slowly the feeling was beginning to return to his hands and his pounding headache was beginning to subside. Although groggy and thinking he should go home, he really wanted to find out who the mystery man was and where he had gone, and figured it had to have something to do with the base. Having warmed up sufficiently, he made his way back to where he had been left to die. He followed a set of ski tracks out of the woods, across the base perimeter road to the fence and could see where a hole had been cut. He made his way back to his truck and drove to where the fence had been cut and parked, leaving the engine running. His throat was parched and he really needed a drink. He searched around in the truck and found an old used paper cup, which he filled with snow and held next to the heater blower until it melted into ice water. He repeated this process several times until he had quenched his thirst. Wolf thought he would wait a little bit longer and got comfortable, putting his feet up on the bench seat and propping his head up on a rolled-up hunting jacket. Soon he was asleep in the warm cab.

\* \* \* \*

By now, the community of Foxhollow was feverish with the Fuller brothers' story about the flying saucer and Wolf's disappearance. The talk in Morgan's Bar and Grill, just after noon on that Saturday, was that Wolf had been abducted by Aliens. Wolf's girlfriend, Carol, was asking the Fullers what they remembered and not surprisingly they could barely remember anything that had happened after they had left work at the tractor plant yesterday afternoon. Carol had gone to public and high school with the Fuller brothers and knew they were good people, but these days they drank too much. Her father, Gil, had been very good friends with Larry and Mike's father, Greg, up until his untimely death in a snowmobile accident a few years ago. Since then, Gil had been like a father to the boys and often invited them and their mother, Sybil, over to join Carol and his wife, Sarah, for a barbeque during the warm summer months. The Fuller brothers were in their early twenties and had been born less than a year apart. They were both single and still lived at home with their mother. Larry, the older and taller of the two brothers, had long dark hair which was frequently hidden under a Minnesota Twins baseball cap. He had bright eyes and a long thin face and was wearing a thick dark brown leather jacket over a dirty looking suit vest. His brother, Mike, had long dirty blonde hair, blue eyes and a kind of California surfer look. He was wearing multiple layers of shirts under a greasy looking dark blue ski jacket. The Fullers had grown up in Foxhollow and in their later years at school had both excelled at cross-country running. In their last year, they had represented the northern Minot schools region at state track meets in Fargo and Bismarck, but neither of them had finished in the top twenty.

"I'll tell you what I remember "said Larry in a dry raspy voice. "It had been a real late night at the Bird and on the way home, we saw a flying saucer. Wolf stopped his truck for a while and we watched it move across the sky, right Mike?"

"Yea, that's right," said Mike. "I saw it plain as day."

"Do you have any idea what happened to Wolf?" asked Carol, bursting into tears.

"I remember he dropped us off outside our house," said Larry.

*   *   *   *

Williams now had to get out of the silo. He already knew from his training that the maintenance door was the only way in and out and it would very likely be locked on the outside. The original plan had been for him to remove the padlock, and enter the silo. But having arrived when the door was unlocked and having nowhere to hide, he felt he had no choice but to enter. He hadn't noticed the padlock at the time. He checked the hinges and they were welded to the door. He banged at the door with the small axe, but it just slipped off the metal. Panic began to set in. He was entombed with a nuclear missile that was going to detonate within less than seventy-two hours. Realizing it would be impossible to leave through the maintenance door, he began to investigate if there was any other way out. He couldn't see any other doors on the level he was on and because the lower levels were further below ground, he figured it was highly unlikely he would find a way out down there either, but checked anyway and as expected, found only solid steel and concrete all around. He knew there was no way to stop the detonation countdown and if he wasn't able to get out before the explosion, at least his death would be instantaneous. However, he still had lots of time ahead of the planned Monday afternoon detonation, so his panic gradually began to subside and he began to focus his attention on the large silo cover above the missile.

He thought to himself that if he hadn't damaged it so badly, he may have been able to open it and leave that way. While looking up at the large cover, he noticed a smaller cover, off to one side. He climbed up a wall-mounted ladder and studied it. He figured it would be padlocked on the outside but the hinge attaching it was visible and was attached with very large screws. Williams figured he should be able to remove the screws and unhinge the cover, so he climbed down and using the small axe, sliced into a number of storage lockers, until he found some toolboxes. He searched around inside them and found a very large screwdriver, a hammer and vice grips. He climbed back up the ladder and using the screwdriver, tried to remove the screws, but none of them would budge. He fastened the vice grips around the handle of the screwdriver, held it up to one of the screws and hammered at the vice grips. Using this method, he managed to loosen and remove two of the large screws, but the others seemed to be rusted to the hinge. He climbed back down and smashed into some more storage lockers until he located a power drill and some assorted drill bits. After linking several extension cords together, he climbed back up and was able to slowly drill out the centers of the other large rusted screws. He then pushed the small, but surprisingly heavy, cover up and out of the way. He climbed back down the ladder one last time, retrieved his backpack, climbed back up and squeezed out through the small hatch into the bright sunshine. It had taken him almost two hours to break out of the silo and it was just before two o'clock in the afternoon; he was several hours behind schedule.

\*   \*   \*   \*

At Morgan's, Biff told Carol that he and some of Wolf's friends and neighbours were going to look for him.

Carol grabbed her coat. "I'm coming too."

About a dozen men and Carol came out of Morgan's and jumped into their cars, trucks and vans.

"Follow me," shouted Biff, leaning out of his truck window. He led the convoy out onto the road that led to the base.

Carol and Larry were riding with Biff.

"You know, it must have something to do with the base. Most things around here do," said Biff.

The convoy soon reached the northern perimeter road.

"Look in the snow banks and ditches," said Biff.

There wasn't much to see apart from snow-covered trees. When they reached the western end of the northern perimeter road, they turned south. About fifty minutes later, they had reached the western entrance to the base. Biff pulled over to the side of the road and jumped out of his truck. Those following in the convoy also got out of their vehicles. They gathered around Biff and he told them he was going to talk to whoever would listen to him on the base, about the Fullers' story and told them to wait here for him. Biff got back into his truck and turned into the base entrance, stopping beside a guardhouse. A young man in an Air Force uniform greeted him and asked if he could help him. Biff said he needed to speak to someone about an incident near the base, earlier that morning.

"Do you have ID?" said the guard.

"Here," said Biff, handing him his tattered old wallet "Take whatever you want - driver's license, Medicaid card, whatever."

"I mean base ID," said the guard, pushing the wallet back towards Biff.

"No, I don't, but I still need to talk to someone."

The young airman, seeing Biff was becoming visibly agitated, told him to wait while he made a phone call. He went to the back of the guardhouse and called through to the base headquarters building. He had a short conversation with someone on the other end and came back to the window.

"Someone is on their way to talk with you. Please go back and wait in your truck."

After quite a while, a Jeep pulled up next to where Biff was parked. Biff got out of his truck and a clean cut, uniformed officer asked him if he was the person who had something to report and introduced himself as Major John Lang, of the United States Air Force.

"Yes," said Biff. "Early this morning, three young men from Foxhollow saw a flying saucer moving towards the base and one of them has disappeared. That's it. I just thought someone on the base should know."

"I haven't heard of anything unusual happening today, but I will report this to the base commander. Could I please have your name and phone number?" asked the major.

"They call me Biff and my last name is Morgan. I will write my phone number down for you." said Biff, snatching the notepad out of the major's hand.

"Thank you for the information," said the major, retrieving his notepad from Biff. "I guess we'll keep looking for our friend," said Biff, shaking the major's hand.

Major Lang drove back to the base headquarters building and informed Base Commander William S. Maty about the information he had just been given. After he had finished, Will Maty, chuckling, commented that usually he read about these kinds of things in the local supermarket checkout line.

"Nothing out of the ordinary has been reported, but I'll check with the tower to see if they noticed anything unusual and get them to check their logs. You say this guy seemed believable?"

"Yes. He had a small convoy with him."

"Quite strange," said the base commander. "Leave it with me, Thank you, Major."

After the major had left, Base Commander Maty got up and walked over to look at the Minot Air Force base emblem hanging on the far wall of his office. There was an M, followed by a missile representing I, then an N. Following the N was what looked like the head of an old wild west Cavalry officer representing the O, followed by a T. When he was troubled, he often looked at the base emblem for inspiration. He wondered what this was about.

\*   \*   \*   \*

Biff led the convoy back the way they had come north, then east, along the northern perimeter road, until they came to the road back to Foxhollow. It was starting to get dark. They had found no trace of Wolf or his truck. Little did they know that if they had turned east instead of west on the northern perimeter road, when they had first started out, they would have found Wolf and his truck within a matter of minutes. Larry had slept most of the way home, so Carol hadn't been able to get any new information from him.

\*　\*　\*　\*

Once he was out of the silo, Williams quickly got his bearings and made his way to where he had buried his ski equipment. He found the orange garbage bag, put his work boots in the backpack and put his ski equipment on again. He shouldered the automatic weapon, checked his compass and began to head in a northerly direction, across the barren, snow-covered landscape. After skiing for a while, he remembered as a youngster reading about the native Plains Indians who had roamed these lands during the winter months and began to visualize a train of them far off in the distance. He could see multi-coloured ponies, pulling what he thought were called travois. There were a number of older men, chiefs he guessed, at the head of the train, followed by warriors of all ages and behind them lots of women and children. They were all wearing long colourful fur cloaks and he could hear the children laughing as they played. Still in the moment, he thought about what he had just set in motion and although it wouldn't bring their way of life back, it may make their ancestors think back to the way things used to be a hundred or so years ago.

Williams almost slipped on a rough patch of icy snow and lost the mirage. He was thinking how under circumstances of total isolation, the mind was capable of amazing things. He thought to himself that whenever he reached his Shangri-La, he would try and cultivate this amazing phenomenon. As he was making his way off the base, he was unaware that a local search party was looking for the man he had left for dead, earlier in the day. He was now primarily thinking about meeting up with Shelby at the ski resort and how late he already was. He was finding the skiing quite tough and was doing his best to keep up a steady pace. He kept checking the compass to ensure he was still heading north. One thing he had going for him was that the weather conditions were clear, even though he had a biting wind to contend with.

* * * *

A number of miles north-east of the military base, Peter Shelby was waiting at the southern border of the Ebdon ski resort. After returning to the farm and letting everyone know that the drop had gone well, he had managed to get a few hours' sleep before starting out for the resort. As General Tsoff or Major Khotov - he couldn't remember which one - had predicted, his vehicle had been thoroughly searched at the border. He had compensated for this eventuality by leaving the farm several hours early. He and his vehicle were now on file with US Immigration and Customs. He had indicated to them that he was going skiing at the Ebdon ski resort, which was true. Once across the border, as he was merging onto Interstate number 83, he realized he'd crossed the border here before. The interstate ran north from Bismarck to the Canadian border. He had been fishing up in Manitoba with his father on several occasions when he was a teenager.

He arrived at the resort just after eleven. He took his overnight bag and ski equipment inside with him, leaving Williams' bag in the Bronco. When he got to reception, he found out that he and Williams had pre-paid rooms for the night. He planned to meet up with Williams around noon.

\* \* \* \*

Wolf came awake just after three-thirty in the afternoon. The truck's engine was not running and he felt quite cold. He figured he must have woken up at some point, turned it off, then dozed off again. He decided he would go home, thinking his girlfriend must be worried sick about him. He took one last glance at the base perimeter fence and noticed something off in the distance. After locating his high powered hunting binoculars, he could see a skier off in the distance coming his way, so he waited until they got closer. He waited until he could see the skier pushing his way through the fence, then grabbed his hunting rifle, jumped out of his truck and ran towards the fence.

As Williams was squeezing through the fence, Wolf recognized him and shouted, "Drop the weapon and put your hands up."

Williams looked up and recognized Wolf, too. With all the problems he'd had in the silo, he'd completely forgotten about the encounter earlier that morning. However, it all came back to him in a hurry now.

"You again? Let me get through the fence first," he said angrily.

"Yep, it's me again," replied Wolf. "Figured you'd left me for dead, did you?"

William's mind was already working a mile a minute.

"Listen," he said, collecting himself. "I'm on a military mission, testing the base security."

"What are you talking about?" said Wolf, looking confused. He moved over to where Williams was standing and hit him square in the face with the butt of his rifle. Because Williams was wearing sunglasses, the blow shattered one of the lenses, cutting him above the left eye. His nose also started to bleed, blood dripping down into the snow.

"There! I owe you that. Maybe I'll leave you to die out here; how would you like that?" said Wolf.

When Wolf hit Williams, he'd been knocked back but he hadn't fallen, and with his back to Wolf, had pulled out his pistol. He swung around and pointed it at Wolf's head.

"Drop the rifle!"

Williams cleared the blood from his face with his jacket sleeve, leaving a red smear across his face. He told Wolf to go and get in his truck. He picked up Wolf's rifle, along with his own automatic weapon, and as he was walking towards Wolf's truck, he asked him what he was doing out here.

"I saw the flying saucer and wanted to know what was going on," said Wolf.

"As I told you," said Williams, "you are interfering with a United States government top secret mission."

Once they got to the truck, Williams ran around and jumped into the passenger seat, pushing the pistol into Wolf's face as he climbed up into the drivers' seat. Williams asked Wolf if he knew how to get to the Ebdon ski resort from here and when he said he did, told him to drive there as quickly as he could. Williams told him he was going up to the resort for a debriefing meeting on what he had found out about the base security. Wolf still didn't know what to think about the situation.

"I'm Gerry," said Williams. "What's your name?"

"They call me Wolf."

On the way to the resort, Williams threw his automatic weapon and a number of items out of his backpack into the snow-covered trees as they sped by. He also threw Wolf's hunting rifle into the trees, much to his dismay.

While they were making their way up to the resort, Williams couldn't believe what a talker this guy, Wolf, was! In the half hour it took them to get to the resort, he had heard his whole life story. He apparently liked to hunt and snowmobile in the winter, fish and camp in the summer, and always went to the Indy 500 on Memorial Day weekend. He was currently living with his girlfriend and her two children, in a rented house, in a town called Foxhollow, west of here. He had grown up in St Cloud, just north of the twin cities of Minneapolis/St Paul and had got into trouble with the law at an early age. He had married young and had always had difficulty holding down a regular job. Several years back, with warrants out for his arrest, his marriage falling apart, he had decided to make a clean break and had headed up the interstate to Fargo. In Fargo, he worked for a number of different courier and delivery companies, and after a year or so of scraping by, living in subsidized housing, had moved further upstate to Grand Forks. He had only stayed there for a few weeks, due to the lack of employment opportunities and a shortage of subsidized housing. Since moving west to Minot, his luck had changed and things had really started to work out for him. On his first day in Minot, he found an assembly line job at an agricultural equipment manufacturing plant, the largest employer in Minot apart from the Air Force base. The company had found him rental accommodation in Foxhollow and he had met Carol and liked her so much that he had willingly accepted her children as part of the package. He had been living happily with her and her kids ever since. The last year had been the best of his life so far and he was seriously thinking about putting down roots.

Williams had forgotten what people who stayed close to home were like. He still knew people he had grown up with in upstate New York who had stayed close to home. He realized it was only when you left home and travelled that you became "worldly", as they say. This guy, Wolf, was the normal one of the two of them, with his simple life. It was him who was now different. He had left home over a decade ago and become very independent, living a life that could in no way be termed simple. He had now become national, if not international, but had never really realized it, up until now. *Yes*, he thought, *this guy Wolf is the normal one, not me. It's true what they say about never being able to go home again.* Just as he was having this thought, they arrived at the resort.

\* \* \* \*

It was getting late into the afternoon and Shelby had already consumed a hip flask of Scotch in an effort to try and keep warm. It was beginning to snow and get dark. He scanned the bleak snow-covered landscape along the northern edge of the base. Williams had obviously been delayed, but he figured they still had plenty of time to get their return flight. Right then, though, he needed to get back to the resort lodge before nightfall.

When Shelby got back to the lodge, he went up to his room, changed and went down to the lobby bar where he couldn't avoid getting into a conversation with the perky young barman. The barman said he had never seen him there before. Shelby's training had not included how to make small talk, which he had never been good at. He thought about it for a second or two, and said he was from Bismarck and hadn't come this far north to ski before and was meeting a friend down from Canada. The barman didn't pursue the fact Shelby was from Bismarck, as he was not from North Dakota himself and didn't know much about the cities in the state. Seeing Shelby was not much of a talker, he didn't bother with him anymore and got busy collecting empty glasses and loading them into the dishwasher.

Most people were still on the floodlit slopes and the resort was very quiet. Shelby could hear the old standard, "Moon River" playing, which took him back to his childhood when he was growing up a hundred miles or so south of here. Although he'd had a fairly normal upbringing, he felt that by living in Bismarck, he had missed out on the pop culture of the sixties. TV and radio had been the only way he could enjoy any of it. He remembered his parents often listened to tunes like this.

He had gone to the local schools, followed by college, up in Minnesota. He had majored in advertising and because he was naturally creative, had done very well. So well in fact, that he had been snapped up by a top advertising agency in New York City after graduation. When, a number of years later, an opportunity to work in their London office had come up, he'd jumped at the opportunity, thinking he could make up for the lost sixties. He remembered the words from a Roger Miller song, "England swings like a pendulum do," but instead, upon his arrival had found the city to be dirty, dingy and lacking in even basic amenities. He had thought to himself at the time. *You obviously had to have been here back then.*

Now as he sat there at the bar on a cold North Dakota winter afternoon, he just hoped that General Tsoff would be true to his word when they got back. His old life hadn't been so bad and if he hadn't decided to go to Moscow, he probably would have returned to the States once his current assignment had been completed. Anyway, now he hoped he would end up somewhere warm and tropical, with lots of toys. Although he knew he had been chosen to play a lesser role in the mission, he felt he had already made a significant contribution, flying and dropping Williams off, returning to the farm without incident and now being at the ski resort to meet up with Williams. He knew that the general had taken an immediate liking to Williams and that he was much more of a take-charge kind of person than himself. Only one of them could set the missile warhead detonation process in motion and it was fine with him that Williams had been chosen. He was now, however, starting to get concerned about Williams' whereabouts and wasn't quite sure what to do. He decided he would have another drink and if Williams hadn't shown up by the time he had finished it, he'd phone Major Trsenkov.

After finishing his drink and paying his bill, he phoned the farm from a public phone in the lobby, using the long distance calling card Major Trsenkov had given him. The major suggested he should go to his room in the resort and wait for Williams to show up. The major figured Williams would likely meet up with him very soon and asked Shelby to call him in an hour if he still hadn't shown up. Otherwise he would see them at the farm tomorrow. Shelby did as the major had suggested, went to his room and took a shower.

Major Trsenkov thought he would wait and see if Shelby phoned again before informing General Tsoff that Williams had not shown up at the resort yet. He knew that once the general heard there was a problem, he would spend a great deal of time analyzing all the possible scenarios and he wasn't feeling very well at the moment. He also knew from previous experience that he would only end up with more work to do. He had to be careful though, because if Williams didn't show up, the general would want to know why he hadn't been informed earlier. The major checked his watch; it was almost twenty minutes past four. He wondered what could have delayed Williams; surely he couldn't have been caught. Perhaps he'd hurt himself somehow or maybe everything had taken longer than planned. He began to think whether there was anything he could do. Should he send agents out to look for him? But given it was almost dark, it didn't make much sense to do this. He figured the best thing he could do was sit tight and wait and see if Shelby phoned again.

\*   \*   \*   \*

Biff was back behind the bar at Morgan's. His regular customers were all still there, discussing the Fuller brothers' flying saucer story. In a quiet moment, Biff called the local police station to inform them of Wolf's disappearance and ended up completing a missing persons report.

"You know, Mildred," he said to his wife, "Wolf is still out there somewhere. I don't think even the Martians could get the better of him. I'm sure he'll turn up, aren't you?"

Mildred, the ever-agreeing spouse, indicated her concurrence by nodding her head as she moved off to serve some newly arrived customers.

\*   \*   \*   \*

The lodge was quite an impressive structure, built from large logs with white caulking between them. It gave it the luxurious look of other lodges Williams had seen numerous times in travel magazines. It looked as if it could accommodate a significant number of overnight guests. As they made their way towards the entrance, Williams pointed to the large hunting knife strapped to his leg and said to Wolf, "I know you're a nice guy and all that, but cause me any trouble in here and I'll cut you real bad, no kidding. We're going to the bar as soon as we get inside."

They went in through the main entrance and over at the reception desk, they could see someone behind the counter, talking to a group of skiers. Williams looked like a nondescript appliance repairman, having ripped off all the Soviet paratrooper badges from his uniform. Wolf looked like a backwoodsman. The few people they could see were all wearing brightly coloured sweaters and pants. There was a full-sized stuffed bear just inside the door, which Wolf told Williams was a grizzly. To Williams, it was just a big bear; he couldn't tell the difference. Williams was amazed how big it was, at least eight feet high, with large, scary looking claws and teeth.

They manoeuvred their way through a number of wooden lacquered tables and chairs on the way to the bar.

There were several moose and deer heads mounted on the wall behind the bar. They sat at the bar, facing the end wall of the lodge, with the lobby reception area at their backs. They were the only ones sitting at the long bar. There was a young barman behind the bar who seemed reluctant to serve them, until Williams smoothed him over, saying they were meeting someone and wouldn't be there long.

"I guessed you boys weren't here for the skiing, but as far as I know, we don't have a dress code," commented the bright-eyed barman. "What can I get you?"

Williams ordered two shots of whiskey and two beers and when they came, quickly downed his whiskey and took a sip of the beer. He reached into his backpack, brought out a hundred dollar bill and handed it to the barman, who didn't show any surprise at being handed such a large bill. Williams grabbed his backpack and when the barman came back with the change, picked it up leaving some small bills. He stood up, moved away from the bar and told Wolf he was going to the washroom. After going to the washroom, he went to the reception desk and asked which room Peter Shelby was staying in. The women behind the desk said she couldn't give out that information, but if he would like to go over to one of the lobby phones, she could put him through to Mr. Shelby's room. Shelby answered the phone almost immediately.

"Guess who!" said Williams. "What's your room number?"

Williams quickly found the room. Shelby had lots of questions about what had delayed him.

"It took me hours to start the detonation countdown and get out of the silo, but we need to get out of here right away. Get your things and let's go!"

"But I thought we were staying here tonight?" said Shelby with a puzzled look.

"The situation has changed, we need to get out of here as quickly as we can, I'll explain the reason later".

On their way across the resort parking lot, Williams opened the hood of a truck and pulled a handful of wires and cables off their housings. He threw them into the back of the Bronco as he got in.

"That should slow him down."

"Who?" said Shelby.

"I'll tell you about that later too," said Williams laughing.

They left the ski resort driving north.

It seemed like a long time since the paratrooper had gone to the washroom and Wolf, having finished his whisky and beer, was wondering whether he should order another round, even though the paratrooper's beer was still almost full. He decided instead to go and look for him. He wasn't in the washroom and coming out, Wolf looked over to the bar and he still hadn't returned. He looked around the lobby and couldn't see him anywhere. After looking along each of the hallways leading from the lobby and still not seeing him, he went to the reception desk.

"Have you seen the guy in white coveralls that came in with me, a little while ago?" he asked the receptionist.

"Yes, I just saw him leaving with another man a few minutes ago. You might still be able to catch them," she said.

Wolf rushed out into the parking lot and saw a vehicle turning out into the road. It was dark, but he could tell it didn't have North Dakota license plates. He ran and jumped in his truck, but it wouldn't start. He got out, lifted the hood and saw that the battery cables were missing. He kicked one of the front tires, hurried back into the resort, found a phone and dialled 911. After giving his name, he was surprised when the operator told him he had been reported as a missing person. Wolf began to tell his story and the operator immediately interrupted him and told him someone would be coming out to the resort to speak with him very shortly.

When Williams and Shelby came to the first crossroads, they turned west. Williams reached into his backpack, took out a pill bottle, shook out some stamina pills and swallowed them. He asked Shelby if he wanted any and when he declined, put the bottle back into his backpack. Shelby asked him if they were going back to the farm. Williams said he didn't think it would be a good idea to cross the border right now, with a guy back at the resort who knew he'd been on the base. Shelby was very puzzled by this.

"Let's keep going west for now. I think we should try and find somewhere to stay for the night; we've still got plenty of time."

As Williams was changing into the ski clothes Shelby had brought for him, he was thinking about adding an additional twist to their current situation - picking up some women. They were passing through a small town when he noticed a country bar set back from the road.

"Can you do a U-turn? I think we should get off the road for awhile and the bar back there looks like it might be a good place to kill a few hours."

A few minutes later, they were walking towards the door of a bar that looked about as country as you could get. On the way through the door, Williams was telling

Shelby why having women along with them could be of great help.

*    *    *    *

Not very long after Wolf had called 911, a police car arrived at the resort. Standing out in the parking lot, Wolf told the police officers about the flying saucer, the guy who had jumped him and left him to die, and who had forced him to bring him up here to the resort. He showed them the skis in the back of his truck and the ski shoes inside the truck's cab. Wolf told them that the paratrooper had thrown his automatic weapon and some other things into the trees along the side road on the way up to the resort. He told them that he had also thrown his hunting rifle into the trees and he was planning to go back to look for it when his truck had been repaired. One of the police officers told him if he found any of the things that had been thrown into the trees he should take them to the closest police station. The police officers asked Wolf to come into the resort with them. When they got inside, the officers asked the receptionist if someone had recently left the resort in a hurry, with another man. The receptionist confirmed that a man wearing coveralls had left in a hurry not long ago.

"He looked like some kind of repairman," chipped in the young bartender, who was cleaning off a nearby table.

"Him and that guy came in about an hour ago," he said, pointing at Wolf.

"Thanks; we may need to talk to you again later," said one of the police officers. The officers talked to the receptionist for awhile and then asked Wolf to come back out to the parking lot with them. They told him they were taking him to the local police station to put a description of his abductors together, and asked him to get in the back of their patrol car. Wolf told them he could only give them a description of the guy who had forced him to drive him up here. He said he hadn't seen the other person or their vehicle up close. He had only seen tail lights and an out-of-state license plate, but didn't see the number. The police officers ignored him and as they pulled out of the resort parking lot, one of them was talking into a citizens band radio, requesting a tow truck to come and pick up Wolf's truck.

*   *   *   *

As they came through the door, Williams and Shelby could see they were in an authentic country and western bar. There were bear, big horn sheep and a multitude of other wild animal heads mounted on the walls and a country and western singer was whaling out a sad tune on the jukebox. Williams rapidly took the place in and was surprised by the number of what seemed like unescorted women - at least five or six. Surely he and Shelby could get lucky in here, even though they seemed to have a problem based on the looks they were getting. It must have been obvious to everyone in the bar, that they were strangers, their bright ski clothes standing out from everyone else's drab jeans and leather jackets. Their clothes would have been fine at the ski resort, but here they looked totally out of place. Williams suggested that they should at least take their ski jackets off. He could see there were some really good things about the bar - no TV's, a loud juke box and a few people already dancing off to the end of the bar.

The bartender leaned over towards them and said, "You boys just passing through?"

"We're down from Canada, doing some skiing and partying," said Williams loudly, hoping that this would explain their inappropriate clothes to anyone within ear shot. Williams had become the spokesman for himself and Shelby, as Shelby normally shied away from interactions with other people. Williams didn't have a problem with this as he was naturally outgoing and enjoyed meeting people.

"Are there any motels close to here?"

"On the other side of town, you'll find the Moonlight," chipped in the sexy bartender's assistant.

"We'll check it out later, thanks," said Williams. "Two Buds please."

The cold beers were quickly passed their way.

"Cheers!" said Williams clinking Shelby's beer. "You know, I was just thinking, I don't remember any discussions with the general on what would happen if things really went wrong."

Shelby asked Williams what had happened to him since he had jumped out of the plane, which now seemed like a long time ago.

"Well, to say things got off to a bad start would be an understatement. The jump went well and I was setting off for the base when some guy hiding in the woods tried to jump me. Can you believe it? Someone was out there in the woods, at four in the morning? What was that all about? Anyway, I'd seen him while I was unpacking the supply package, so before he knew what hit him, I'd knocked him out cold. Later I found out he recovered."

"Surely General Tsoff hadn't arranged this?" said Shelby.

"No. This guy was a just a curious local."

Just then, three women who looked to be in their late twenties, came into the bar. They made their way to a vacant table next to the makeshift dance floor; one of them was extremely attractive.

Williams continued, "I got to the silo just about on schedule; however, that didn't go exactly as planned either. It turned out there was a maintenance crew inside. Because I had nowhere to hide outside, I foolishly entered the silo. In hindsight, I should have waited for them to leave and then gone in. When the crew left, they locked the only door in and out of the silo, on the outside. Setting the detonation process in motion went relatively smoothly, although I was pretty shaky and had a few problems. It was when I came to get out of the silo that I had major problems. I tried, but couldn't break out through the door. After about almost two hours, I finally managed to get out through a small opening at the top of the silo. I skied off the base and as I was squeezing through the perimeter fence, guess who was waiting for me? Yes, the same guy who had tried to jump me earlier in the morning. Eventually I got the better of him for a second time, getting a bloody nose and a nick above my left eye in the process, and forced him to bring me up to the resort."

"Who was this guy?" asked Shelby.

Williams continued "I don't have a clue. He said his name was Wolf. It turned out that he had seen the plane-flying saucer come over and hover, saw the parachutes open and wanted to find out what had landed. Gutsy guy really. Anyway, let's hope that's the last we've seen of him."

Little did Williams know that only a mile up the road from where they currently were, Wolf was on the phone talking to his girlfriend, telling her he was at the Tollesbury police station. While he was talking to her, he saw a tow truck, with his truck in tow, go past the window. Carol was telling him not to worry, because Biff and the Fullers were on their way to get him. Once he got off the phone, he was given some forms and asked to write out a statement and provide a description of the paratrooper. As he was completing these, Biff and the Fullers came bursting into the police station and were told that Wolf would be with them soon.

When Wolf came out the interrogation room a few minutes later, he saw Biff and the Fullers. He handed the statement and description to the duty officer and asked if it would be alright if he left his truck overnight and he would come back and get it in the morning. The duty officer agreed and Wolf, Biff and the Fullers left.

Looking around the bar, Williams said, "Let's see if we can find someone to spend the night with." He asked Shelby to move along to end of the bar, closer to the makeshift dance floor. "So who do you fancy?"

"The sexy young girl behind the bar; how about you?" said Shelby laughing.

Williams checked his watch. They had been in the bar for almost an hour now and he figured it was time to make a move. He walked over to the table where the three recent arrivals were sitting and asked the attractive blonde if she would like to dance.

"No thank you, not right now. We're waiting for our drinks to come, but you and your friend are welcome to join us, if you like," she replied.

This friendliness surprised Williams and he waved to Shelby to come and join him while he was asking the people at the next table if he could take one of their chairs. Shelby, carrying their ski jackets, the backpack and beers, joined Williams at the table with the three women.

"Hi, I'm Gerry," said Williams.

"I'm Peter," said Shelby.

The women's drinks arrived and Williams asked the waitress to put them on his bill. He raised his beer saying "Cheers" and they all clinked their glasses and beers together.

The blonde said, "I'm Jill and these are my friends Sylvie and Vi. We rent a house together."

Vi didn't seem to be very tall; she had short black hair and a pale face. She was very well dressed in a black leather skirt and a white fluffy blouse. Sylvie appeared to be quite tall and slender and was wearing a tight-fitting slinky light blue dress. She had a friendly face and was quite animated when she talked. She seemed to be the glue between the women. Jill, a natural blond, was by far the most attractive, with a very pretty face and jaw-dropping cleavage displayed to its best advantage in a pink low cut wool sweater, accented with a short black skirt and a pair of black and white high heels with a fifties look to them.

None of the women looked very country and with Williams and Shelby sitting with them, their group looked out of place in comparison to everyone else in the bar. Williams, with his rugged good looks and five o'clock shadow, looked like one of the models who advertise men's grooming products. Shelby, with his handsome good looks, also stood out from the crowd. Their table looked like an island of chic in the middle of a sea of leather and denim.

Sylvie asked the men where they were from. Williams said they were down from Canada and had been skiing at the Ebdon ski resort and that they were planning to stay the night somewhere close by and head home in the morning. He said they were from Winnipeg, even though neither he nor Shelby knew much about the place. It seemed to be the closest big city up in Canada. This immediately led to some awkward moments when Vi said she had lived there at one time. Williams let Shelby answer the questions about where they lived and did they know so and so. Williams was thinking how clever General Tsoff had been to have sent them on the mission. Soviet agents would have stood out like fish out of water in a place like this.

Williams heard Roberta Flack starting to sing "Stromin' my pain with his fingers, singin' my life with his words" and whispered to Shelby that he should ask Sylvie to dance. He touched Jill's arm and asked her if she would dance because, he said, he really loved this song. She jumped up to dance. Shelby asked Sylvie and once they got on the dance floor found out she was a pretty good dancer.

When they sat back down and started talking again, Sylvie said the girls all worked together in the billing office of a local power company. Williams described himself as an investment advisor and Shelby as being in advertising. Jill said she could use some investment advice and Williams gave her a rudimentary overview of investment options, from savings accounts to speculative penny stocks and everything in between. Jill seemed most impressed with him.

Williams had to admit with her pretty face and voluptuous figure, Jill looked most enticing. Already after only the one dance, he knew she would do whatever he wanted, it seemed like she couldn't get enough of him. Shelby, on the other hand, being nowhere near as smooth as Williams, was struggling to make the right connection with Sylvie. His natural shyness wasn't helping the situation, but when they danced, she felt really good in his arms.

As the evening progressed, the bar filled up and the lights were dimmed. It was so busy now that Williams and Shelby were no longer being noticed. After several beers, Williams was beginning to feel light headed and realized he'd been up since two in the morning and hadn't eaten anything all day. He got the attention of one of the busy waitresses and ordered nachos for the table. Already knowing the chemistry was right between him and Jill, he now wanted to ensure Shelby got paired up with Sylvie. He had taken an immediate dislike to Vi and wondered if her name was short for Viper. Williams danced exclusively with Jill while Shelby danced alternately with Sylvie and Vi, much to William's annoyance. He noticed again how impeccably dressed Vi was and thought maybe she wasn't really that bad. They were sitting back at the table when Vi checked her watch and said she had to leave to meet someone and asked Jill and Sylvie if they would get ready to go.

"Are you girls leaving already?" said Williams with emphasis, trying his best to act surprised and disappointed.

"Afraid so," said Sylvie. "We came in Vi's car."

"We could give you a ride if you like, right Pete?"

"How long are you guys staying?" enquired Jill.

"As long as you want," said Williams.

"Anyway, I really have to go," said Vi, putting her coat on.

Williams could see that Jill wanted to stay, but Sylvie wasn't sure. Jill, sensing the same thing, asked Vi if she could wait a minute and asked Sylvie to come to the washroom with her. When Jill and Sylvie returned, Jill told Vi that she and Sylvie would get a ride with Gerry and Peter. Vi, looking somewhat hurt, thanked Williams for the drinks, said her goodbyes and left.

\*   \*   \*   \*

Wolf, the Fullers and Biff drove straight to Morgan's, where Wolf's friends and neighbours were still gathered. Wolf told his story to anyone who was interested and although the Fullers and Biff had already heard it on the way back from the police station, they were listening just as intently as everyone else, hearing it for the second time.

"No, I wasn't abducted by Aliens; sorry to disappoint you all. Apparently I got mixed up in a military exercise, testing the base security. I never did find out why they were using an aircraft disguised as a flying saucer - all part of the testing, I guess. I did meet the paratrooper involved in the exercise, who thought I was there to stop him. I don't know if you know, but he knocked me out cold and I didn't come around for a number of hours. Another hour or so more and I could have died from exposure!"

Biff interrupted him. "You know, we went to the base looking for you and they didn't tell us anything about any exercise."

"Apparently, it was top secret," Wolf replied, "so they probably couldn't mention it or maybe they didn't even know about it.

"I waited around for a few hours and then met up with the paratrooper again as he came off the base and then took him up to the Ebdon ski resort. He said he had a de-briefing meeting there but soon after left with another man for some reason.

Biff interrupted him again. "Don't you think it's strange that he would be having a meeting about a top secret exercise at a public ski resort? You'd think he'd be having the meeting on the base."

"Maybe he didn't want the base to know about it - he was testing the base security after all. Anyway, I'm here with you all now and no harm has come to me."

Carol noticed that Wolf's eyes were beginning to close and asked their next door neighbours if they could get a ride home with them. Biff told Carol that he would take Wolf to get his truck tomorrow morning before he opened the bar. Wolf and Carol left with their neighbours. The Fullers left right after them, saying they were tired too and needed an early night.

$*$ $*$ $*$ $*$

Less than a hundred miles from where Williams and Shelby were sitting in the country bar, Captain Bradley Wilcox was driving in through the main gates of Minot Air Force base. As he drove onto the base, he passed a large sign that read, "The Proud Home of the United States Air Force 5th Bomber Wing and 91st Missile Wing." He was working the ten-to-six shift that Saturday night. He always liked to get to work early, so he could have a coffee and a smoke before starting his shift. He was coming off two weeks' vacation and was in an excellent frame of mind. As one of the launch control facility operators, Wilcox had a security pass that allowed him to go anywhere on the base. Tonight he was working Charlie flight of Bravo squadron at the north end of the base. His job was quite mundane and very repetitive - the way you would expect a job to be after you'd been doing it for more than twenty years. He felt like a glorified night watchman, even though he was minding some of the most potent weapons ever invented by mankind. There were continuous checks to be done and frequent launch readiness tests, known to everyone on the base, as LRTs. The technology involved was now rather outdated and although the missiles were automatically monitored, operators were still required to note and report any anomalies. Significant incidents with the missiles had been very few and far between over the years, the most serious having been the first year the missiles were installed. A missile's main engines started up and it was in the process of lifting off before they were shutdown. Obviously, the initial LRTs had been a little too realistic and extensive damage was done to the almost launched missiles silo. There had also been a number of false alarms over the years, mainly due to feed pipes or sensors freezing up, but the almost-launch was the only real major incident. Wilcox, originally from Chicago, really enjoyed the outdoor activities North Dakota offered. During the fishing and hunting seasons he would go off with his friends into the remoter parts of the state for several days at a time. He found these trips to be very challenging and enjoyable. Although his job at the base was not particularly difficult, it was stressful, knowing the awesome power of the weapons for which he was responsible. A number of operators had cracked up over the years, becoming alcoholics or even committing suicide. Minot, North Dakota was a pretty god-forsaken place, especially during the cold winter months. Due to the lack of sun in the winter, it was almost as if night turned into night again. Although the Air Force paid these keepers of the peace very well, it was difficult to attract and keep people for very long at Minot. Wilcox was an exception.

Wilcox, like most operators, rotated through a different flight every week and a different squadron every two months. This allowed him to work each flight within a squadron at least once before taking two weeks off. He worked all five Minutemen squadrons and the new Peacekeeper squadron each year. This kind of schedule was fine with him. Although the launch control facilities were identical, each week tended to be different, depending on the LRTs that were scheduled. This week he and his partner were scheduled to perform a number of LRTs on the Charlie flight missiles. Upon his arrival at the Charlie flight launch control facility that night, he headed for the small lunch room. It had a sink, counter top, table, chairs, coffee making machine, microwave and a full size refrigerator. Hanging over the sink was a rack of coffee mugs, all bearing the insignia of SAC. Wilcox poured himself a cup of coffee, sat down and was just lighting up a cigarette, when his partner, Captain Mike Green, strode through the door.

"Hi Mike, how are you tonight?" asked Wilcox.

"Good, thanks. Did you hear they're having all kinds of problems with the new control system over at the new Peacekeeper squadron? One of the operators told me they almost let one off last week. Some kind of software glitch."

Wilcox said he hadn't heard anything.

Green poured himself a cup of coffee, sat down opposite Wilcox and asked him what was on the agenda tonight.

"LRTs with SAC."

"Great!" said Green sarcastically. "That's all we need, those geeks from SAC breathing down our necks."

"They're only doing their job," replied Wilcox.

\*   \*   \*   \*

Williams and Shelby danced Jill and Sylvie through a marathon of sad country love songs until Sylvie said she wanted to leave to catch one of her favourite sitcoms. Shelby and the two women put their coats on and made their way out to the icy parking lot. Williams stayed behind to pay the bill and then joined them. The others were already in the Bronco when Williams caught up with them. Sylvie was in the front with Shelby, so Williams joined Jill in the back.

"Hey, why don't we get some beer and go over to the Moonlight Motel?" he suggested. "I understand it isn't far from here and I'm sure they have TV's in every room."

"Sounds like fun to me," said Jill, squeezing Williams' arm. "It's still quite early."

Sylvie said she still wanted to go home.

Williams nudged Jill.

"Oh come on Sylvie, let's have a little more fun tonight," Jill said.

Sylvie thought about it for a few moments and reluctantly agreed, saying "Can we hurry then, so I don't miss my show?"

"Great!" said Williams and asked Jill if there was a gas station on the way.

Jill said she thought there was one just up the road. Sure enough, it was about a mile up the road, next to a police station. Williams ran in and grabbed two six packs of beer.

When they got to the motel, Williams went into the office and paid in advance for two adjoining rooms for one night. When they got into one of the rooms, Sylvie ran over, turned the TV on and flipped the dial until she found her show. Williams gave Shelby a plastic ice bucket and asked him if he would mind going to get some ice.

"What would you ladies like to drink? A beer or a beer or a beer?" asked Williams jokingly.

"Beer please," they both shouted.

"Two beers coming right up! I think you'll need to drink right out of the can - the plastic glasses in the bathroom are real small."

Both women said the can would be fine and Williams pulled two off the plastic carrying ring, passing one to Jill. He walked over to where Sylvie was sitting and handed her the other one. Just then, Shelby came back with the ice and Williams put the remaining cans into the sink in the bathroom and threw the ice on top of them. He handed Shelby a beer and got one for himself. Shelby went and sat at the end of one of the beds next to Sylvie and Williams bounced onto the bed next to Jill, hitting her can with his saying, "Cheers!"

"You know, if I'd thought about it, I would have bought a pack of cards," said Williams.

Turning around, Sylvie said, "I don't play cards."

"So how about we just talk?"

"You go ahead," said Sylvie. "I'm watching my show, thank you."

Jill asked Williams if he'd ever been skiing around there before and he said he hadn't.

Shelby, being more forward than usual, whispered to Sylvie that when the next commercial came on would she like to watch TV in the other room with him.

A few minutes later, as Shelby and Sylvie were approaching the adjoining room door, Williams said, "We need you ladies to stay with us tonight. I promise we'll take good care of you. Pete obviously can't drive anymore - he's had too much to drink."

"We can get a taxi," responded Sylvie immediately.

"No, you are staying with us tonight, end of discussion," said Williams firmly.

Sylvie burst into tears.

"Look," said Williams, "Don't make this harder than it already is."

Sylvie moved towards the door and said, "Oh no? Just watch me."

Williams jumped up, blocking her way and pulled his pistol out of his backpack. Pointing it at her he shouted, "Move away from the door or I'll shoot you and I'm not kidding!"

Sylvie backed away staring at Williams in horror.

"Now ladies please try and relax. We don't want to hurt you," said Williams.

He reached down, pulled his sheathed hunting knife out and handed it to Shelby, saying, "Here. If she tries anything, cut her."

Shelby and Sylvie, who was still in shock, went into the adjoining room.

*Jill is amazing,* thought Williams. *She doesn't seem to care at all about what's going on; it seems all she wants is sex!*

When they got into their room, Shelby apologized to Sylvie and asked her if she would stop crying.

"I don't care who you people are; just don't hurt us," said Sylvie, still weeping.

Shelby turned on the TV, found her show and she calmed down. After about half an hour there was a knock on the adjoining room door.

"Can I come in?" asked Williams.

Shelby opened the door.

"Here" said Williams, handing them each a can of beer. "Sylvie, I'm sorry, but you will have to be tied up" he said, ripping long strips from a linen bed sheet.

"Why don't you let me tie her up?" said Shelby.

"Sure, no problem," Williams said, handing the bed sheet and the strips he had already ripped off to Shelby. "You take care of it."

Through the open adjoining room doors, Shelby could see Jill lying on the bed, with her hands and feet tied together. He figured Williams had already had his way with her and he was beginning to really dislike him.

"Goodnight. Sweet dreams," said Williams, leaving the room.

After finishing her beer, Sylvie said, "I'm ready to go to bed."

"Where do you want me to sleep?" asked Shelby.

"With me and will you please make love to me before you tie me up? You seem like such a nice man," she whispered.

"If this is a trick, forget it. I have the knife right here," said Shelby, waving it in the air.

"No, I mean it! I promise I won't try anything," pleaded Sylvie.

They both got undressed, slid into bed and turned off their bedside lights.

\*　　\*　　\*　　\*

It was exactly ten o'clock on Saturday night when Captains Wilcox and Green took over from the two operators at the Charlie flight launch control facility.

At the same time Wilcox and Green were starting their shift over at the base headquarters building, Technical Sergeant Sven Jacobsen was completing his. Jacobsen worked in the scheduling department and was responsible for planning the launch readiness testing rotations. He had made a number of subtle scheduling changes over the last several months to ensure that the missile in one of the northernmost silos, Bravo Charlie missile number four, would not be undergoing LRTs during the time that Major Trsenkov's software modifications were being made. He thought the major would be very pleased with the work he'd done. Jacobsen had been recruited while he was on a fishing trip up in Canada several years earlier. He had met the major at a time in his life when he had been at his lowest. He had been taking the trip to try and take his mind off his serious financial problems. He had even contemplated committing suicide but had been too chicken. He knew that running into the Soviet major had not been a chance encounter and later learned that the Soviets had been trying to find someone on the base to work with them for quite a while.

The launch control facility where Wilcox and Green worked was shaped like a hexagon, with distinctly different compartments. Two of the compartments had identical racks containing rows of switches and small status lights. There were multiple phones on either side of these racks. The controls in these compartments would be used in the event the order was received to launch missiles. Both operators would enter the launch codes simultaneously. There were also test simulators and control equipment in these compartments. The two adjacent compartments were taken up with all kinds of gauges, small and large. These were visually monitored on a continuous basis to ensure any malfunctions with any of the missiles or associated equipment were immediately noted and reported. The remaining two compartments were usually locked and contained the controls that would be used once the missiles had been launched. Each launch control facility had the capability to launch any flight of missiles on the base, to ensure that if a particular launch control facility was taken out by an enemy strike, its missiles could still be launched. During their shift that night, Wilcox and Green would be performing LRTs on Bravo Charlie missile number one. They were early into their shift when the phone rang and Wilcox was informed that a maintenance crew had discovered that Bravo Charlie missile number four's silo had been infiltrated. The head of base security told Wilcox that the maintenance crew would be phoning in again soon with another update. He told him that all LRTs were to be suspended indefinitely. Wilcox informed Green, and the engineers from SAC working with them, about the news.

# CHAPTER 4

***Sunday February 14***

Further examination of Bravo Charlie missile number four's silo in the early hours of Sunday morning revealed that the main silo cover's hydraulics and a small silo service cover had been damaged.

*   *   *   *

The automatic wake-up message on the phone in Williams' motel room rang and rang just after six o'clock Sunday morning. He eventually answered it and although he felt dog tired, dragged himself out of bed. He walked over and banged on the adjoining room door, shouting that it was time for Shelby and Sylvie to get up. Jill, woken by Williams' shouts, looked over at the clock and asked why they were getting up so early.

"Pete and I have a plane to catch," said Williams moodily.

"What?"

Williams realized he'd goofed and said, "Don't worry about it. I'm going to take a quick shower; then I'll untie you and you can use the bathroom."

Sylvie, woken by the banging and shouting, asked Shelby what time it was. Shelby said he didn't know but felt as if he'd just gotten off to sleep. "Sit tight. I'm sure Gerry will be in here very soon telling us exactly what to do."

"What do you mean? What to do?" asked Sylvie. "I thought you were taking us home today?"

"Just relax" said Shelby.

The shower in William's room stopped and a few minutes later there was a knock on the adjoining door.

"Can I come in?" asked Williams.

"Hold on" said Shelby, as he moved to unlock the door.

Williams burst into the room dripping wet with a towel wrapped around his waist. "Get ready. You've got time to take showers if you like."

"Why are we getting up so early?" asked Sylvie.

"You'll find out soon enough," said Williams, leaving the adjoining room door open as he left the room.

A few minutes later, Williams came back into their room fully dressed and asked Shelby for the keys to the Bronco. Shelby grabbed them off the bedside table and tossed them to him. Sylvie couldn't see Jill, but could hear the shower going in the other room. She saw Williams carrying a pile of folded sheets and blankets across the room and heard the room door open. This puzzled her greatly.

Within an hour they had left the motel. Williams still believed that the authorities would not be looking for two couples. Once they turned out onto the highway, Williams waved his large hunting knife at the women and told them he would use it if they didn't keep quiet if they were stopped by the police.

"Why would we be stopped by the police?" asked Sylvie.

"I heard there are two escaped convicts on the run," said Williams.

Sure enough, within ten minutes they came to a police roadblock. The state trooper could see that their vehicle had province of Manitoba license plates. He approached the driver's side of the Bronco and asked Shelby where he was headed and where he was coming from. Shelby said they were on their way back to Canada and had been visiting some friends in Minot. When asked where they were from in Canada, Shelby said Winnipeg. The trooper put his head in the window and asked Williams and the women if they were also from Winnipeg and they all said they were. This seemed acceptable to the impeccably dressed trooper and he let them pass through the roadblock.

\* \* \* \*

At first light on Sunday morning, two of Base Commander Maty's senior officers went to inspect the damaged silo. They found there were already a number of people inside when they got there. They were shown the damage to the main silo cover hydraulics and could see that a lot of oil had dripped onto the missile's nosecone. They learned that an axe had been used to do the damage and were told the cover couldn't be opened until the hydraulics had been repaired. They were shown the hole where a smaller cover had been removed and were also shown the newly installed alarm override panel, which had obviously been installed to stop alarm alerts from being sent, but nobody knew why yet.

Major Scott Waltham and Lieutenant Colonel Graham Smith left the silo and began to look for any clues the intruders may have left outside. They made their way to the silo security fence and found the metal frame surrounding a hole in the fence. They soon figured out that it had allowed someone to crawl through without setting off any alarms. *Quite ingenious!* thought Waltham. Close by, they found an empty orange garbage bag partially buried in the snow. They put on their ski equipment and began to follow a single set of ski tracks. After following the tracks for miles, they reached the base perimeter fence. They skied along beside it until they found a hole cut in the fence. The tracks they had followed seemed to indicate that there had only been one skier on the base. On the other side of the fence it was a different story. There were numerous footprints and fresh tire tracks in the snow. It seemed the skier had been picked up by an accomplice. Before setting off, Waltham had arranged for a base security patrol vehicle to pick him and Smith up and within fifteen minutes, it had arrived.

\*    \*    \*    \*

It was now just after seven o'clock in the morning and Williams knew they would be coming to the border soon. He'd already decided the border could be a completely different proposition from a police roadblock. They might be allowed to go through without incident because they were couples but any other scenario could mean big trouble. The women probably had identification, but this would be confusing because they were Americans. Also, who knew what they would say if they were questioned individually? And what would they do with the women once they got across the border? Williams didn't think they could take the gamble and started to look for a trail leading into the forest. They hadn't gone far when they passed one and he asked Shelby to do a U-turn and take the trail into the woods, to his surprise. As they drove down the trail, numerous leafless tree limbs brushed against the Bronco's windows. Once the trail began to narrow, Williams asked Shelby to stop. Using strips of bed sheets, Williams tied the women's hands and feet together. While he was doing this, he asked Shelby to lay blankets out on the ground in front of the Bronco. Jill was her usual calm self and Williams thought he would really have liked to have spent more time with her. Sylvie, on the other hand, was pleading with Shelby not to leave them there. Williams carried them one at a time and laid them down on the blankets and Shelby covered them up as best he could. Williams told the women that once he and Shelby had crossed the border into Canada, they would let the authorities know where they were, so they shouldn't worry too much.

As they backed up along the trail, Williams told Shelby he was dumping the women because he didn't know what they'd do or say at the border. Shelby didn't look happy and knew now that he definitely didn't like Williams. Seeing the unhappy look on Shelby's face, Williams said, "Don't worry. They'll be fine; they're warmly dressed, covered with blankets and it's not supposed to snow until tonight."

They soon reached the border and were informed by the border guard that all vehicles with out-of-state license plates were required to check in with Canadian Immigration and Customs and asked them to drive over to the Customs building. Williams, knowing they couldn't be detained because the authorities would have a description of him by now, leaned over and quietly whispered to Shelby that they needed to get out of there pronto. Shelby, although reluctant, launched the Bronco into the wooden barrier blocking their way, splintering it into pieces and sped off up the hill leading away from the border crossing. They were definitely on the run now and every cop in the area would soon be looking for them. Now that they were in Canada, Williams wondered if the US authorities could touch them. They had only traveled a few miles when they could see flashing lights up ahead in the distance. Williams figured it was probably a police roadblock and the border police could only be minutes behind them. He asked Shelby to take the next trail into the woods that they came to. They soon reached one and Shelby drove down it, over several large fallen tree branches, crossing a frozen creek. The trail came to an abrupt end, overlooking a spectacular view of massive rocks on the side of a deep gorge. Williams told Shelby to back up and drive along beside the frozen creek. They came to an overhanging weeping willow and Williams told Shelby to drive under it, stop and turn the engine off. Under the willow tree, the Bronco was well hidden from the trail.

Two border police patrol cars had reached the police roadblock and were being informed by Canadian police that no vehicles coming north from the border had been stopped. The Canadian police told them that several minutes earlier they had seen headlights approaching from the south off in the distance, but they had disappeared. While they were talking, another Canadian police car arrived. Officer Gettis, who seemed to be in charge, said he would check the trails between there and the border and suggested the border police, return there in case they were needed. He asked the newly arrived police officers to take over the roadblock.

Williams and Shelby had been parked, talking quietly for almost twenty minutes, and had not seen or heard anything. Shelby was concerned that they were running out of time to get back to the farm.

Officer Gettis was following the fresh tire tracks on the trail Williams and Shelby had recently driven down until he was stopped by a fallen branch. Not being able to get over it in the police car, he backed up the trail and stretched out several lengths of yellow *Police Line Do Not Cross* tape across the entrance. He called dispatch and asked them to arrange to have some heavy moving equipment sent to where he was located as soon as possible.

After waiting another ten minutes or so, Williams and Shelby agreed that if they were going to get to the farm on time, they needed to keep moving. Shelby drove out from under the willow tree in the opposite direction from the trail and almost immediately found his path blocked by a rotting tree trunk.

"Let's start hiking. They'll be looking for the Bronco anyway, not us," said Williams, grabbing his backpack.

They made their way over numerous fallen trees, following the winding creek northward. Williams knew they needed to get to the road and hitch a ride.

\* \* \* \*

At the Tollesbury police station just after nine o'clock on that Sunday morning, Wolf had discovered that so many cables and wires had been ripped from under the hood of his truck, he would need to have it repaired by a mechanic. He told the duty officer he would have to arrange to have it towed to a service station in Foxhollow and asked if he could use the phone.

\* \* \* \*

As they came out of the woods, Shelby mentioned that they needed to call the police about the women. Williams, somewhat agitated, said he hadn't forgotten, but there didn't seem to be telephone out here in the woods. After standing in the trees off to the side of the road for quite a while, they heard a truck approaching from the north. A huge logging truck came barrelling around the bend, heading straight towards them. Although it was heading south, Williams figured it might be the only chance they might have of getting a ride before the police caught up with them.

"Quick, go down like you're hurt!" said Williams. "I'll try to get him to stop."

Williams ran out into the road, in front of the approaching truck, waving his arms wildly. He immediately heard the *pssst* sound as the truck's air brakes were applied and heard the rumbling sound coming from it's chassis as it came to a stop further up the road. Williams sprinted to it, climbed up onto the running board and opened the truck's heavy passenger door. He told the burly tough-looking driver that his friend was hurt and needed medical attention and asked if they could get a ride to the nearest town. The driver told him to hurry up and Williams waved to Shelby to come and join him. Shelby limped as quickly as he could to the truck and Williams pulled him up into the cab beside him.

*   *   *   *

Waltham and Smith reported their findings to Base Commander Maty. The base commander said he was concerned about the damage to the main silo cover and during their debriefing, phoned the Minot police chief explained the situation to him and told him where to start the search for those responsible for damaging the silo on the base. The base commander informed his officers that while they were gone, there had been an incident at the border crossing directly north of the base which might well be connected to the break-in.

*   *   *   *

By now Officer Gettis, with the help of a bulldozer, had located the deserted Bronco and phoned in the Manitoba license plate number. He had found what looked like two overnight bags, ski equipment, some white coveralls, some cables and a pair of work boots in the back of the Bronco. The Bronco had been traced to a car rental company in Winnipeg and the records showed that it had been rented several days earlier by a Mr. Davis, whose address in Brandon, Manitoba didn't exist. Gettis arranged for a tow truck to come and take the Bronco in for a forensics examination. He had followed two sets of footprints in the snow out to the forest road and it looked like whoever they belonged to had hitched a ride south. He guessed by now he was several hours behind them, whoever they were.

\*   \*   \*   \*

At the border crossing, Williams and Shelby could see a lot of commotion. Outside one of the buildings there were six or seven police cruisers parked at different angles, all with different emblems and lettering on their sides. There were two covered army trucks parked to one side of the police cars and a number of the soldiers were standing smoking and talking.

The logging truck driver indicated to the border guard that he had a passenger who needed medical attention and was told to go and check over at the US Customs building. The driver checked with Customs and it turned out that the closest emergency facility was ironically in Minot. So that's where they were headed, until Williams spotted a motel up ahead and asked the driver to drop them off there. Williams said he would ice his friend's injury and get a taxi to the hospital in Minot if it didn't get any better. The logging truck driver obliged him even though he felt somewhat put out and dropped them off outside the Elk Motel.

As soon as they got into their room, Williams phoned 911 and told the operator where to find the women. When he was asked for his name, he said, "You need to find them as quickly as possible," and hung up. Shelby hoped the women would be alright and wondered if there might have been any wild animals in the woods. He didn't think Williams had thought about that or likely cared. He remembered there were many wild animal heads mounted on the walls of the country bar they had been in the night before. He was still very unhappy about the way Williams had treated the women. He turned on the TV and could only get two snowy channels, one showing "I Love Lucy" and the other "The Beverly Hillbillies".

"Should we phone the farm?" asked Shelby.

"No. I don't think that would be a good idea. I think the mission plan will have changed by now. They will probably already know that the police authorities are looking for us. I know how people like them think; they will want us dead now. There is no way we can go back to Moscow now. But this might be the best thing that could have happened to us. Do you really think General Tsoff would have set us up for life, in a place of our choosing, anywhere in the world? I've thought about that a great deal and it wouldn't have happened. It is much more likely they would have shot and buried us right where we'd been killed."

"You're probably right. If they could force us to do this, they could do anything to us," agreed Shelby.

\*　　\*　　\*　　\*

Technical Sergeant Sven Jacobsen had arranged to meet with Major Trsenkov on Sunday morning at a family restaurant several miles south-west of the farm. He had crossed the border into Canada, at a different border crossing from Williams and Shelby, without incident and was already in the restaurant when the major came in and sat down opposite him. The major didn't appear to be very happy, which disappointed Jacobsen because he thought he had done a good job.

Major Trsenkov passed Jacobsen an envelope under the table and whispered, "I'm sure you will be very pleased with our generosity, but please don't open the envelope until you get home."

Jacobsen stashed the envelope inside his jacket. They talked about the news and weather for several minutes, after which the major got up and left the restaurant. A few minutes later, Jacobsen was out in the parking lot unlocking his car when he suddenly felt a terrible pain in his side. He had been shot twice from close range with a gun with a silencer. He dropped his car keys, went limp and was caught as he fell by two of Major Trsenkov's agents. They dragged him over to the major's dark sedan and dumped him in the trunk. Before he closed it, the major reached inside Jacobsen's jacket and removed the envelope he had just given him. He knew Jacobsen was just starting his days off from work and lived alone, so it would be awhile before anyone missed him. His body was going to be taken to the farm and buried. An agent driving Jacobsen's car followed the dark Lincoln sedan out of the restaurant parking lot.

*   *   *   *

When the Americans failed to show up at the farm, it presented a dilemma for Major Trsenkov because it had been planned that he would be joining them on their return trip to Moscow. General Tsoff apparently wanted the major back in Moscow in the aftermath of the explosion. The major phoned the general with the news. General Tsoff asked him to change his flight to tomorrow and rang off.

Soviet agents monitoring local police transmissions already knew about the incident at the border and figured it had to be Shelby's Bronco as it was too much of a coincidence not to be. Some agents had already been dispatched to find out what they could about where the Americans might be. They were dressed like hunters and when they stopped at the police roadblock just north of the border, were surprised how much information they were able to gain about the ongoing search for the two men who had crashed the border. It seemed they had abandoned the Bronco in the woods, just north of the border and had hitched a ride south. This new information was quickly relayed back to the farm.

\* \* \* \*

In addition to Jacobsen, the Soviets had informants working in the North Dakota highway patrol central dispatching office and the Minot police department. They had already reported that the damaged silo had been discovered. These informants had been singled out as being most vulnerable to threats to their loved ones and were under threat that one or more of their family members would be harmed if they didn't cooperate.

\* \* \* \*

Sunday afternoon, after reading Wolf's statement and speaking with the officers who had brought him in, Tollesbury Police Chief Gordy Wilkins, commented that he wasn't sure about the flying saucer at the beginning but thought the end seemed real enough, as there was no other plausible explanation for this guy to be at the Ebdon ski resort. In addition, some of the resort employees had seen both him and the man in the coveralls. One of his officers phoned the base and informed them about Wolf's statement and was told the information would be passed on to the base commander. As it turned out, it would be several days before Base Commander Maty would get the message and by then he knew all about the problems with Bravo Charlie missile number four.

*   *   *   *

At the Elk Motel, when the six o'clock news came on, there was no mention of anything going on at the Air Force base. The lead story was about a homicide in a downtown Minot hotel the night before. Some other nondescript news was followed by the local weather forecast.

While Williams and Shelby were watching the news, a state trooper was in the Elk Motel office asking the owner who was staying there. The trooper learned that two men had checked in a few hours earlier and were the only ones currently staying there. He asked the owner to call the police station if the two men showed any signs of leaving.

Upon returning to the station, the trooper reported the information to the duty officer. Knowing the Elk Motel was situated very close to the border crossing where an incident had occurred earlier in the day, the duty officer insisted an arrest warrant be obtained to bring the two men in for questioning. A patrol car was dispatched to get a warrant for the arrest of the two men on suspicion of crashing the border.

*   *   *   *

At the Elk Motel, Williams and Shelby were discussing their next move.

"We obviously need to get as far away from here as we can, as quickly as we can," said Williams.

"You know," said Shelby, "I'm getting to know this area pretty well. I've been through the same border crossing three times in the last two days. We could go to my parents' place; they only live about a hundred miles south of here."

"Think about it; do you really want to get your parents mixed up in this? I'm pretty sure the general's men are trying to catch us to kill us. Do you want your parents killed too?"

"I thought I could warn them about the explosion," said Shelby.

"Nobody can know about it, not even your parents. Its better they don't know and especially about your involvement in the whole thing!"

"Who are you to decide this?" said Shelby angrily.

"All I'm saying is, this is our problem, nobody else's. Let's keep it that way. Your parents should be fine. Why didn't you mention them before?"

"It only just occurred to me," said Shelby, still angry.

"Check with them after the explosion." said Williams. "So we agree, we don't want to go south towards the base and we don't want to go north through the border crossing again, so it just leaves east or west. I personally think west is our best bet, because it's much less populated. Are you alright with this?"

"I guess so," said Shelby sulkily. "Should we take the interstate?"

"No, I don't think that would be a good idea because it's where the highway patrol is much more likely to be and if we break down for any reason, they're more likely to locate us. I think we're better staying on the local roads and highways."

"What about the weather forecast we just saw? Do you think we should be setting off when there's so much snow forecast?"

"We don't have a choice. If we don't keep moving, either the police or the Soviets will catch up with us. I'm sure of it. If the weather conditions are bad, it will be the same for everyone. I'll go and see if I can find us some wheels," Williams said, leaving to go to the motel office.

\*     \*     \*     \*

Just after seven o'clock on Sunday evening, Williams and Shelby set off on the journey westward. It was already snowing lightly. Williams had made the motel owner an offer he couldn't refuse, paying him two thousand dollars for a pickup truck that wasn't worth more than a few hundred. After leaving the motel, they filled up at the first gas station they came to. The motel owner had told Williams the truck was great on gas and he sure hoped so. He had given Williams directions west and they soon reached State Highway 5. It was snowing heavily now and visibility was reduced due to the blowing snow.

\*     \*     \*     \*

Once the truck he had sold to the two strangers had pulled out of the motel parking lot, the owner phoned the number the trooper had left him. Very soon afterwards, two state troopers arrived and were not at all happy when they heard the men had already left the motel. They took descriptions of the two of them and the particulars of the truck. They radioed in the information on the suspects and the vehicle, and an All Points Bulletin was immediately put out to the highway patrol. They were asked to be on the lookout for a dark blue, half ton, GMC Cheyenne pickup, license plate number DGTYH.

*   *   *   *

At the same time the state police learned that Williams and Shelby had left the Elk Motel, so did Major Trsenkov's agents, monitoring local police communication frequencies.

*   *   *   *

Shelby was not very impressed with the old pickup truck Williams had purchased. The bench seat's upholstery was ripped and springs were pushing through everywhere. It also sounded like the muffler or tail pipe had a hole in it.

"How far do you think we'll be able to get in this old crate?"

"The guy at the motel said it had been a great runabout truck and had never let him down."

"I hope he's right, because if it breaks down, we could be in big trouble."

"Let's cross that bridge when we get to it and anyway don't you know by now my middle name is Trouble? Why don't you try and get some rest so you'll be able to take over the driving later."

"I'll try, but it's a pretty bumpy ride and look at the foam and springs pushing up through everywhere!"

"Yea, I know," said Williams "but these were the only wheels he was willing to sell me. Try not to let it bother you. Think about something enjoyable, like your old girlfriend."

Shelby did exactly what Williams had suggested and began to think about Christina. He wondered what she was doing. For sure it wouldn't be snowing where she was, but it could well be raining though. That was one thing he really didn't like about London; it always seemed to be raining and often drizzled for days. It really restricted the things you could do outside and it was almost impossible to plan any kind of outdoor event. He thought about the parties he used to go to with Christina. She was always telling interesting stories about when she was growing up in Italy, where, from what he could tell, it rarely rained. He was in the middle of remembering one of her stories about jumping off high cliffs into the sea, when sleep overtook him. Williams was pleased when he heard Shelby starting to snore.

It was snowing really hard and Williams was finding it difficult to see past the large snowflakes hitting the windshield. The wipers weren't clearing the windshield very well and were leaving smears of frozen ice. He tried to tune in the radio, but only got noisy static all the way across the dial. He figured either the antenna or the radio must be broken. Shelby had been right about the seat; he could feel something pushing up into his backside and had to move around to find a more comfortable spot. He thought to himself that, with the weather conditions being so bad, it was unlikely anyone would find them out on the roads tonight. He couldn't get the planned detonation out of his mind, but thought for sure he and

Shelby would be forgotten once the mushroom cloud appeared high in the prairie sky.

As they drove west through the raging blizzard, the truck seemed to be holding up well despite Shelby's concerns. It did seem to be good on gas, the temperature gauge was consistently in the normal position and the engine was running smoothly. On the downside, the heater, although working, wasn't keeping the cab very warm. The seat wasn't very comfortable and he couldn't get anything on the radio. Shelby woke up just as they were driving into a gas station at the North Dakota-Montana state border. Williams had been driving for almost four hours and asked Shelby if he'd take over once they had filled up.

As they left the gas station with Shelby driving he could hear Williams snoring softly and realized the driving was up to him now, so he'd have to concentrate. It was still snowing heavily and the visibility was very poor. As he drove on into the night, he occasionally lost control of the back end of the truck and had to slow down until it righted itself. The tires were probably bald and there was no weight over the back axle to help with the traction. If he kept at around fifty-five miles per hour, he found the truck was more stable. They were now in the state of Montana and it seemed to be snowing even heavier, if that was possible. Shelby was also glad that they seemed to be the only vehicle on the road that night.

\* \* \* \*

Just before midnight, information was received at the farm that some agents down from Canada had spotted the beaten-up old truck they had been watching out for at the North Dakota-Montana state border. The Canadian agents had been getting coffee at a gas station, when they noticed an old dark blue Cheyenne pickup truck pull in. Although the license plate was obscured by a build-up of snow and ice, they figured there could only be one of these trucks out on the road tonight. Major Trsenkov told them to just follow it.

# CHAPTER 5

## Monday February 15

As Sunday turned into Monday, Shelby continued to drive west along State Highway 5, until it ended at a place called Scottly. He turned south and drove through a maze of snow-covered county and unpaved roads until he reached State Highway 2, near the town of Glastonby. The snow had almost stopped now and he was able to gradually increase his speed.

\* \* \* \*

Early Monday morning, Major Trsenkov phoned General Tsoff to update him about Jacobsen and the Americans; it was just after nine on Monday morning in Moscow. The general was pleased to hear the news about Jacobsen and said he was confident that the Americans would soon also be dealt with. After the major told him the Americans were heading west, the general asked him to change his plans and follow them west and kill them. He told the major to make sure he got far enough west to ensure he wouldn't be affected by the explosion later in the day. The change in plan was most acceptable to Major Trsenkov, as he now had the opportunity to ask all the agents within a wide area of the base to head west to assist him in the search. This would take them all out of harm's way also.

Once he got off the phone with Major Trsenkov, General Tsoff phoned Major Khotov in Havana, even though he knew it was already after midnight there. When the major answered, the general explained the situation to him and told him to take the next available flight back to Moscow. Since arriving in Cuba, Khotov and the attractive flight attendant had seen the sights of Havana and had made a very attractive couple. Major Khotov said he would look into the available flights first thing in the morning. The general wished him a good flight home and hung up.

*    *    *    *

While Major Trsenkov was discussing the best way to go west with Sam and Anton, General Tsoff phoned him and told him that he had just been given full authority over all of the Soviet agents in North America, so now the major had them all at his disposal. The major thanked him, hung up and went back to planning his trip. He was concerned about crossing the border south of the farm because they would be carrying all kinds of weapons and he was worried their vehicle would be searched as it was not already on file. Sam suggested they stay in Canada and travel west as far as they could before entering the United

Stephen Knight

States. He said this would be faster anyway, because the roads in Canada were better. So it was agreed.

* * * *

Although the Soviet intelligence agency, the KGB, was aware of General Tsoff's mission, it was not until it started to go wrong that they asked to get directly involved. When they found out that the Americans would not be returning to Moscow, they contacted the general. He updated them on the current situation and suggested they call Major Trsenkov and ask him how they could assist him in tracking the Americans down. The general provided the telephone number at the farm.

Just as Major Trsenkov was about to leave the farm, early Monday morning, a senior KGB officer phoned him and told him the KGB would be assisting him to find the Americans. The officer asked the major to keep him updated on his progress.

The call from the KGB was not a welcome development for the major. His previous dealings with the KGB or the Committee for State Security, the Komitet Gosudarstevannoy Besopasnosty, had not been good. He knew they already had a file on him and this situation could well result in another black mark against his name. That is, unless the nuclear explosion still occurred as planned. Having to keep the KGB updated was an additional chore he didn't need right now. The fact that the Americans were on the run was not as a result of anything he had or had not done, but it wouldn't matter in the end. All he knew was that Williams had been delayed, and for some reason the Americans had crashed the border north of the base.

That the KGB had a file on him was not unusual. They had files on many citizens who had come to their attention when, supposedly, investigating matters of national security. The major's file had been clean up until an incident about ten years ago. Sitting in the back of the Lincoln on his way west, the major recalled the incident that had happened almost a decade ago, like it was only yesterday. He had been working on another assignment for General Tsoff that had gone badly wrong. He was dealing with a senior engineer from a top secret military weapons manufacturing facility in Wisconsin. The engineer had been providing specifications for a new, ship-launched missile called the Tomahawk. The new missile was planned to be used by the United States Navy. It could carry a nuclear warhead and deliver its payload with pinpoint accuracy. The major was meeting with the engineer for the third time, in a downtown Chicago hotel, which, if he remembered, was called the Ambassador. Because this was the engineer's third delivery of top secret information, he was expecting to be paid. So far he had not been paid for any of the information he had provided. At the last meeting, the major had foolishly promised him that he would definitely be paid next time. The major had told the general that he thought the engineer was unstable and that they should at least give him some money. The general had argued that he still needed more detailed information before he would pay out the thousands of dollars the engineer was asking for. When the engineer found out that the major didn't have any money for him this time, he became very angry and screaming obscenities kicked out at a closet door, making a large hole in it at the bottom.

"Calm down!" said the major.

"Why don't you have the money?" demanded the engineer.

"My superiors want more detailed information, before giving you any money. I am very sorry."

"Sorry, is that all you can say? I'm risking my life coming here and all you can say is sorry?" The engineer threw the papers he had brought with him all over the room.

"Calm down! I know you're upset," said the major.

"Upset! You people have tricked me. I have made a huge mistake" he shouted loudly.

"No, no, please, calm down. You will get your money. These things are difficult and always take time."

A woman in the room next door had heard a loud bang and could hear a lot of shouting going on. She had phoned down to the front desk and said she thought the people in the next room were fighting. The hotel manager and a security guard quickly came up to the room, knocked on the room door and asked if everything was alright. The engineer, not able to control himself, had run over and opened the door and said, "No everything's not alright!"

He had pushed by the manager and security guard and run down the hallway towards the elevators. He was quickly caught and subdued by the security guard, while the manager was surveying the damage to the door and asking the major what was going on. With the obvious damage to the door and papers marked "Top Secret" strewn all over the room, the manager had told Major Trsenkov he would have to call the police. While he was on the phone with the police, the major had coolly left the room, taken the stairs down out of the hotel and got into a waiting vehicle, which had sped off. While he had been briefly in the hallway, he had seen the security guard trying to cuff the engineer near the elevators. Several years later, the major had heard that the engineer had been found guilty of divulging military secrets and had been sentenced to fifteen years. Trsenkov knew this would have been portrayed negatively in his file, but really, he hadn't done anything wrong. It was the bureaucracy of the Soviet Union's military that was at fault, not him. He had asked General Tsoff to clear his name with regard the incident, but had never received any confirmation that this had happened.

\*   \*   \*   \*

Early Monday morning the chief engineer on Minot Air Force base was informed that a potentially catastrophic problem had just been discovered with one of the missiles. Engineers had been reviewing alarm message logs from over the weekend and to their surprise, had found that Bravo Charlie missile number four was armed and programmed to detonate later that day. Upon receiving the news, the chief engineer immediately informed Base Commander Maty.

The base commander, still half a sleep and in a state of shock, made his way over to his office in the base headquarters building. Following standard escalation procedures, he notified the SAC commander on duty. He explained that the nuclear warheads in one of his Minuteman missiles were armed and due to detonate in just over twelve hours. This information resulted in red alerts being sent out to all SAC and Air Force senior officers. News of the situation quickly moved up the chain of command to the President himself, in his role as Commander in Chief.

Sitting in his brightly lit office, Base Commander Maty began to make a list of what he needed to focus on. So far he had written: evacuate the base and relocate all bomber and transport aircraft. As he was trying to think of other things that needed to be done, his thoughts began to wander and he began to think about his mercurial rise through the ranks of the United States Air Force since his graduation from the Air Force Academy in 1969. He had been a bomber pilot towards the end of the Vietnam War and had achieved the rank of Captain. Two years later, by being in the right place at the right time, he had been promoted to the rank of Major. At the time, he had just been assigned to Malmstrom Air Force base, in Montana, when a vacancy became available as a result of a sex scandal involving several senior officers on the base. Following this, he had shown himself to be an outstanding leader and had progressed to the rank of Lieutenant Colonel in less than two years. There were many changes in the United States Air Force after the Vietnam War ended, with many senior officers retiring. This created an abundance of opportunities for young, ambitious Air Force officers. Having further proven he had the skills to assume higher responsibility, he had been promoted to the rank of Colonel, when he was appointed the commanding officer of the two active United States Air Force Wings at Minot Air Force base in North Dakota.

Suddenly realizing his thoughts had been wondering, Maty began to think about the crisis at hand. He really felt he needed more information about what he was dealing with here and decided to phone an old friend. A number of years back, he had spent several months at the Department of Energy's Los Alamos, New Mexico, facility and had become friendly with one of the technical directors there, Dr. Jim Swann. He found his numbers and phoned him at his home. When Jim answered, Base Commander Maty already knew he would be able to learn all he needed to know about what he was dealing with here at the base.

"Hello Jim, its Will Maty. Remember me?"

"How could I forget you? What's up at this hour of the night?"

The base commander asked him to swear he would keep their discussion secret. Swann told him whatever it was about, not to worry and swore no one would ever know about their conversation. The base commander explained the situation to him and Swann told him he would do his best to tell him what he thought he needed to know.

Swann began, "The Minuteman III missile has a yield of hundreds of kilotons and if one explodes, it will very likely directly impact anything within a radius of five miles. Like most conventional bombs, most of the damage tends to be done by the explosive blast, except with a nuclear explosion, a much larger area is eventually impacted. When a nuclear bomb explodes, sudden changes in atmospheric air pressure occur, which results in everything in the immediate vicinity being crushed. Tremendous winds, up to five hundred miles an hour, are created, which will uproot trees and snap utility poles. You may have seen the famous films, taken during early nuclear tests, which provided visual evidence of the crushing effect of the winds generated by the blast. In addition to the immediate blast, there will be radiation contamination. Radiation around the immediate blast area will be extremely intense and is commonly known as direct radiation. Fallout radiation is when the dust particulates from the debris cloud settle back to earth. It is very similar to the ash that settles after a volcano erupts. The radioactive fallout can be over an area of hundreds of miles".

Maty interrupted him. "Where is the best place to be if you are in close proximity to an imminent nuclear explosion?"

"I would say below ground, away from the initial blast and resultant direct radiation. A crater will be created, but it will be limited in size. Radioactive dust will be shot high into the air above the explosion site, creating the familiar mushroom cloud. After the explosion, it will be necessary to move through the zone surrounding the crater, wearing special suits that protect against the effects of radiation." Swann's voice broke a little as he said, "Will, I know what you're like and I know you will be there right up until you know for sure the explosion can't be avoided, but please promise me, you will get yourself into an underground shelter ahead of the blast. You are only human and can only do so much and you should save your own life."

"Thank you Jim. I really appreciate this. The information you have given me will allow me to be better prepared for the decisions that will need to be made during the next twelve hours and I promise you that I will get myself and my family safely underground, if it is determined the explosion cannot be avoided. Thank you again. We'll either stop the detonation or you'll hear about it on the six o'clock evening news tonight."

The situation on the base right now was by far the greatest challenge he had faced in his career to date. He had already decided to be up front with his officers when informing them about the situation. It was going to be most important not to lose focus in any particular area and he began to try and compartmentalize everything that would need to be addressed in the coming hours. He had decided to focus all of his own attention on stopping the detonation and he began to think about who he could assign other responsibilities to. He would ask Major Waltham to be responsible for the base evacuation, Major Lang the relocation of all the large aircraft and Lieutenant Colonel Smith for all ongoing operational activities. All non-essential personnel in the Bomber Wing could be evacuated and Major Waltham would need to come up with a reason for doing this. He was trying to put the situation into some kind of perspective, but was having difficulty. In approximately twelve hours there could be an unprecedented nuclear explosion a number of miles from where he was sitting. He would have loved to have been able to assemble every man and women on the base and tell them to go home to their families and get them as far away from the base as possible. But he knew the situation couldn't be handled in this way. Firstly, he and everyone else was going to be doing all they could to avoid the explosion, so why create utter panic and mass chaos over something that hopefully wasn't going to happen? Secondly, just the knowledge of what had transpired on the base over the last day would almost have the same affect as if the explosion had happened.

If it became obvious the explosion couldn't be avoided, protocol dictated that although he was expected to continue to oversee all base activities, he was allowed to ensure the safety of himself and his family. He had been involved in fallout shelter drills before and knew that he would have similar facilities in the shelter to those he currently had. It would obviously be a new experience for him and everyone else. No one, to his knowledge, had actually had to live and work in a fallout shelter for any length of time. The one thing he did know for sure was that the United States military would be doing everything possible to ensure that everyone in the shelters got out safely. He assumed the American public would be told it was an accident, to ensure there was minimal panic throughout the country. He didn't have the time or energy right now to try and envisage all the other ramifications of such a nuclear explosion on American soil, but he knew they would be far-reaching.

\*   \*   \*   \*

Shelby had been driving through the night and it was only snowing lightly now. For quite a number of miles now he had noticed headlights in his rear view mirror that always seemed to be about the same distance behind. He thought this was strange, considering the old truck didn't have much power and almost any vehicle on the road could easily overtake it. After going around a long bend, he pulled the truck off to the side of the road. A black, full sized luxury sedan came cruising by and carried on up the road. He waited a few minutes then pulled back onto the road. The agents had seen the truck by the side of the road and continued up the highway until they came to the first intersection. They went about a hundred yards, did a U-turn, turned the car's lights off and waited. Several minutes later, the beaten up old pickup came puttering by. The agents got back on the highway and began to follow the truck again, this time making sure they kept out of sight. Shelby never saw the vehicle again for the rest of the trip, so never gave it another thought.

\*   \*   \*   \*

As Base Commander Maty sat making his list, he was thinking that if a volcano erupts, it is only those living in the immediate vicinity whose lives are impacted. Life goes on normally for everyone else. His mind was rambling and he couldn't stop it. He was thinking that if there is an explosion, it will be interesting to see if life is impacted in the rest of the country. When there was almost a meltdown at Three Mile Island a few years back, life went on in the rest of the country as if nothing had happened. The base commander thought to himself, *Humans are like ants; someone can step on a few of them, but the rest continue to go about their business.*

\*   \*   \*   \*

The President was awoken just after three-thirty on that Monday morning, by his Chief of Staff, informing him about the situation at Minot Air Force base. The President immediately became concerned about all aspects of a potential nuclear explosion. However, he said he didn't want to cause any panic unless it became absolutely necessary and it looked like the explosion couldn't be avoided. He asked to be brought up-to-date on a regular basis and wondered who could be behind this and what could have motivated them to do such a potentially disastrous thing!

Base Commander Maty was contacted by the President's Chief of Staff just after four on Monday morning. He asked the base commander to be available to attend an eight o'clock conference call, being chaired by the Deputy Secretary of Defence. The base commander said he would be available to attend and already feeling a little tired, wondered when he would be able to sleep again.

At five thirty Monday morning, after listening intently to a briefing by Deputy Secretary of Defence, John Craig, on the situation at Minot Air Force base, the President said, "As well as stopping the missile from detonating, we must focus on containment. We must be extremely careful not to create any suspicions among the American people while we are tracking down the perpetrators. We shouldn't mount a large task force. If we bring in helicopters or vehicles with the FBI logo plastered all over them, it will draw too much attention. We must rely on the state and local police authorities, with the FBI supporting them in the background, to find those responsible.

"Ross, I would like you to take charge. I think it's most appropriate for you, in your role as the Chief of Staff for Strategic Air Command." Looking at Deputy Secretary of Defence Craig, the President said, "Are you in agreement with me here John, that Ross should take the lead?

""Yes overall, Mr. President, but I think the base commander needs to be in charge of the hour-by-hour, day-to-day activities. He is the only one who can bring sufficient focus," said Craig.

"Is that alright with you Ross?" asked the President.

"Yes. William Maty, the Base Commander at Minot, is quite capable of taking on such a role," said Strategic Air Command Chief of Staff Ross Callaghan.

"Although I'm very optimistic that collectively we'll find a way to stop the explosion, we must plan for the worst case scenario, so let's start at ground zero. What should we do at the base?" asked the President.

Craig said, "If it is determined that the explosion cannot be avoided, all base personnel should be ordered to seek cover in underground fallout shelters."

"What about those people living in the immediate vicinity of the base?" the President asked.

"Fortunately, it is very sparsely populated around the base; the actual town of Minot has the largest population in the area and most of the people who live there, work at the base. At the same time the base personnel are being ordered to take cover, the state and local police authorities will be notified about the imminent nuclear explosion and asked to invoke area evacuation procedures as quickly as they can. The initial blast should only affect those on the base in the immediate vicinity of the explosion, so there should be time to evacuate people in the surrounding areas."

"I would suggest the Chief of Staff of the Army be responsible for the overall evacuation. The state and local police authorities will need the support of both the regular Army and National Guard" said the President dryly. "By the way, do we have an estimate of how many people could potentially be affected, if the warheads do explode?"

Craig said quietly, "Early estimates from the Department of Energy indicate it could potentially affect in the region of eleven million people. They indicate that the residual radiation or fallout will most likely drift north-east, affecting eastern North Dakota and upstate Minnesota the worst. Some Canadian provinces will also likely be affected."

"So I guess I should alert the Canadian Prime Minister?" said the President.

Craig continued, "The scientists from the Department of Energy have provided a brief, of which you have a copy Mr President. In essence they are saying the direct radiation will be very intensive, but limited in range. The radiation particles from the debris cloud will affect a much larger area and it could take days or perhaps weeks until all the contaminated radioactive particles have fallen back to earth, some of them being brought back in the form of rain or snow. It is likely that for years afterwards, people may die from the complications of being exposed to the resultant radiation."

The President interrupted him. "Can we go back to the evacuation? I was thinking that evacuating people may result in more of them being exposed to the fallout radiation. Would it not perhaps be better to ask everyone to stay in their homes or wherever they are, at the time of the blast? Keep all the windows and doors closed and then use the Army or National Guard to get uncontaminated food and supplies to them?"

Craig said, "I am told that staying in their homes or offices with everything shut up would initially protect them, but eventually they will have to come out and when they do, they will find the whole area contaminated and will have to be immediately evacuated. It is preferred that everyone be evacuated as soon as possible, before all the contaminated radioactive debris and dust particles settle back down to earth. Following the explosion, many of the particles will be up in the stratosphere, so the much wider fallout area will be only partially contaminated initially.

"I see your point," said the President softly. "So let's get ready to mobilize for a full evacuation of the upper parts of the states you mentioned and the lower parts of the Canadian provinces that may also be affected. As I said earlier Matt, I think you need to take the lead here, given it looks like the Army and National Guard will be handling the evacuation. I'm sure the Air Force will also play their part and be involved in airlifting the evacuees, wherever possible. After having looked at the worst case scenario, we know now that we must do all that is humanly possible to avoid the explosion. Ross, I would like you to ensure the Base Commander gets whatever he needs. Thank you all, and God Bless America."

*   *   *   *

Shelby had had to stop on several occasions through the night to clear the build-up of snow and ice on the truck's windshield wipers. Although the truck's heater was working, it had been no match for the blizzard-like conditions they had come through and he had felt cold for most of the night. It was now beginning to get light and it was warming up inside the cab. Shelby could see that the local snow removal vehicles had been busy throughout the night. Snow was piled high on both sides of the road. Williams, who was awake now, was taking in the magnificent scenery of the rugged mountains and vast snow-covered plains.

Shelby, seeing Williams was awake, said, "You know the trip has gone pretty well so far considering the snowy weather conditions we've come through. You were right about the truck."

Williams asked if he wanted him to take over the driving and Shelby said he was alright for now. It was six-thirty in the morning and Shelby was fiddling with the radio. "It doesn't look like the radio works," he said.

"I know. I tried it last night," said Williams. "Maybe we can sing some songs ourselves. Who were your favorite groups growing up?"

"I really liked the Motown sound, the Supremes, Four Tops and the Temptations. I always found their songs wonderfully up-lifting. How about you?"

"For me it was the Beach Boys and Creedence," said Williams, "but I didn't listen to much music growing up. I had one of those, 'Turn that jungle music off' fathers. So what do you want to sing?"

Shelby thought for a few seconds and said, "How about 'My Girl'?"

"Who did that?" said Williams.

"The Temptations of course."

"You start and I'll join in, wherever I can."

Following "My Girl", they sang one of Williams' favorites, "Bad Moon Rising". They both really enjoyed singing the old songs and it passed the time.

*   *   *   *

Just as he was about to join the eight o'clock conference call, Base Commander Will Maty, for some reason, began to think about the local people who had come to the base Saturday afternoon with the story about the flying saucer and their missing friend and wondered if it was somehow connected. He thought it had to be.

On the conference call, chaired by Deputy Secretary of Defence Craig, were the Director of the National Security Agency, Chief of Staff for the Army, Chief of Staff for the Air Force, Chief of Staff for Strategic Air Command,

Commander of Strategic Command, the Director of the Ballistic Defence Organization, Commander of Pacific Command, Commander of Central Command, Commander of the Northern Command and Base Commander Maty.

Deputy Secretary of Defence Craig began. "Gentlemen, we have an unprecedented situation unfolding at Minot Air Force base today and your discretion is essential. I will try and bring you all up to date as best I can on the facts as I know them. Base Commander Maty, please feel free to cut in at any time if I am missing something important.

Over the weekend, a maintenance crew at the base found that one of the silos housing a Minutemen III missile had been damaged. Then early this morning, it was determined that the missile in the damaged silo has been tampered with. Its software has been modified and a prolonged detonation countdown is well underway. If it cannot be stopped by late this afternoon, it will result in the detonation of the missile's three, one hundred kiloton nuclear warheads. I hope I have captured the essence of the situation, Base Commander?"

"Yes, I have nothing to add."

Craig continued, "So let me try and put the situation in perspective. First and foremost, under no circumstances do we want the missile's warheads to explode. Secondly, we need to find those responsible for doing this, as quickly as possible, and just as important as the first two, we must not let any information about this situation get out.

The FBI has already been contacted and will be providing backup support to the state and local police authorities and the President wants Base Commander Maty to remain in charge. He feels he is in the best position to provide the required focus. Base Commander,

I think we should open the call-up for questions, unless you have anything to add?"

Base Commander Maty said he didn't and the Director of the Ballistic Defence Organization asked the first question. "Do we know if any other silos or missiles on the base have been compromised?"

"Can you take this question, please Base Commander?" said Craig.

"No damage has been reported to any of the other silos and a review of the status of all the other missiles on the base this morning showed no significant issues," said the commander.

"So you are saying that the damage and tampering is isolated to just the one silo and missile?" asked the Director of the Ballistic Defence Organization, for clarification.

"Yes, that is correct."

The Director of the National Security Agency requested clarification of the time the detonation was expected to happen and was told four o'clock local time that afternoon.

"If there are no more questions gentlemen, then I would suggest we let Base Commander Maty focus on the situation at hand. Base Commander, please feel free to contact any of us, at any time. Thank you everyone," said Deputy Secretary of Defence Craig, and ended the call.

\* \* \* \*

Immediately following the conference call, Base Commander Maty met face-to-face with his senior officers. He told them that what he was about to tell them should be treated as confidential. He explained the situation to them and tongue in cheek, asked if any of them had any ideas on how to stop the detonation. The silence in the room was deafening. They agreed that an impromptu air raid drill would be the best way to get everyone into the fallout shelters. The base commander said he would be focusing all his attention on stopping the detonation and asked Major Lang to find a base outside the fallout area that could temporarily accommodate Minot's B-52 bomber and C5 Galaxy transport aircraft. He asked Lieutenant Colonel Smith to take care of all ongoing operations and asked Major Waltham to ensure that all non-essential base personnel were sent home. He said he knew he could depend on them all and excused himself, saying he had to set up a conference call with SAC.

Base Commander Maty chaired a ten o'clock conference call with engineers from SAC, representatives from the missile manufacturer, engineers from the base and scientists from the Defence and Energy departments. He told everyone on the call that everything they were about to discuss was confidential and then explained the situation. He said he wanted to know what options were available to stop the missile's nuclear warheads from detonating. A technical director from the missile manufacturer told everyone on the call that he had been contacted several hours earlier and said so far the most promising option was resetting the countdown variable to its highest value. He said this would obviously buy time to allow them to find a permanent fix and he hoped to confirm whether this was possible within the next few hours.

The base commander said, "Time is obviously of the essence here. We need to find a solution sooner rather than later, so I will set up another conference call, for noon." He thanked everyone for attending and ended the call.

Following the call, Base Commander Maty went back to his office where he found Major Lang waiting for him. Lang told him rumours were rampant on the base, with everyone having their own theories on what was going on. Some of the more popular ones were the new President was going after the Iranian Ayatollah, the base was being closed or the United States was going into El Salvador to make sure they didn't become communist, like Cuba. It seemed that readying the B-52's and Galaxies to leave the base had fuelled most of the rumours. The base commander said he wasn't concerned about the rumours because they were so far off-base and asked Lang how the aircraft evacuation was going. Lang told him that unlike the base fighter aircraft, which were always in a state of readiness, the B-52's and Galaxies had to be essentially taken out of mothballs. All but a few of them had a minimal amount of gas in their fuel tanks, having been out of service for several years now, and getting them all fired up simultaneously was proving to be quite a challenge. Extra air and maintenance crews had even had to be brought in on their days off. Bringing additional manpower onto the base at this time was not really what the base commander wanted to do, but given the circumstances, he figured it couldn't be avoided. He could hear the noise from the monster aircraft as they taxied to the fuelling and de-icing stations and figured he would have to use one of the meeting rooms in the basement of the building for his next conference call.

\*    \*    \*    \*

It was just after ten thirty when Williams and Shelby passed a large sign indicating they were entering the town of Cold Water Falls, Montana. A few minutes later, they passed a monument store, set back from the road.

"Look at the size of some of those monuments!" said Shelby. "Can you see that huge cross with life-size angels on either side?"

"It's hard to see any of them; they're all covered in snow."

"Have you ever considered what you'll have engraved on yours?" asked Shelby.

"No, I've never really thought about it before. I thought that was up to others to decide, after you're gone," said Williams.

"Usually it has some kind of meaning, like a famous quote or something personal about you, but I'm no expert on this either."

"Hopefully we won't need them for awhile, whatever we have engraved on them," said Williams laughing.

It was just before eleven o'clock and snowing lightly when they parked the old truck on the main street of Cold Water Falls, a small town in the foothills of the Rockies. Williams suggested they needed a change of clothes and they headed into a men's clothing store across the street. They bought jeans, long sleeved shirts, underwear, socks and winter jackets and changed into the new clothes in the store, discarding their bright ski suits. They then walked up the street and entered a restaurant called Al's.

\* \* \* \*

The agents who had been trailing them all night watched them park and go into the clothing store. Twenty minutes later, now parked a few cars behind the Americans' old truck, they watched them walk further up the street and enter a restaurant. It had been a long night and as they sat parked there, they hoped the police didn't catch up to the Americans before they had a chance to kill them. But their orders had been to just follow them.

\*　　\*　　\*　　\*

Upon entering the restaurant, Williams thought to himself that this looks like a good place to spend the day, at least up until the explosion. The restaurant was almost empty and looked to be a combined restaurant and bar. It had booths on one side and a bar and a number of tables and chairs on the other and at the back there were several pool tables. They slid into a booth towards the back of the restaurant side and ordered the all-day breakfast special. While they were waiting for the food to come, Shelby began to talk about his ex-girlfriend for some reason. He said she was originally from Italy, Milan, he thought, but she had been working in London for a number of years. She was the manager of a shoe store, located close to Piccadilly Circus, which he likened to the Times Square of London. He said she was very attractive and spoke broken English, with a fabulous accent. He said although he'd been ready to make a long-term commitment, she hadn't. "She'd said she was happy with her life the way it was and marrying an 'Americano', as she called me, would only complicate it. I had only known her for six months, but she was anyone's dream girl. She had it all - looks, brains and a real zest for life. I really miss her a lot."

"Why are you telling me this? I thought it was over?" said Williams, just as their food was arriving.

"I don't know. It's just that I do truly love her," replied Shelby.

"You never know - maybe she feels the same way about you, now you're apart."

"I really hope you're right."

"What's her name?" asked Williams, with his mouth full.

"Christina. I truly hope you meet her one day," said Shelby.

"I can't say I've ever met anyone like her from the way you describe her. Has she got a sister?" said Williams while wiping some egg off his face with his napkin.

"She does, actually," said Shelby. "However, she still lives in Italy and I've never met her."

"You know, I had a foreign girlfriend once," said Williams. "In my final year at Syracuse I dated an exchange student from Egypt and she had a sexy accent too. It would never have worked out between us though, because she said she found America lacking in class compared to Egypt, if you can believe that? Maybe her father was a Sheik or something. Anyway, I honestly think she only dated me to improve her English. She was never comfortable with the American way of life because I think she was already too set in her ways. She was like a celebrity wherever we went, so I know exactly what you mean about women with fabulous, foreign accents."

Al thought it was very unusual for anyone to stay in his restaurant after eating breakfast and figured the two strangers must be killing time or lying low for some reason. He could see them playing pool at the back of the bar and walked back to where they were and asked them if he could get them anything.

Williams checked his watch. It was almost noon and he said, "Well it's almost afternoon; I think I'll have a beer, how about you, Pete?"

"Sounds good to me."

Al came back with the beers and asked them if they were just passing through or staying in town.

Williams replied, "We're passing through, on our way to see some of my relatives, out on the west coast. This was all he could think of on the spur of the moment. We've been driving all night and need a little down time. Us being here isn't a problem, is it?"

"No, no problem, not at all," said Al. "Stay as long as you like and if you need anything, just holler. I'm Al by the way."

"The Al of Al's restaurant?" asked Williams.

"Yes, that's me, in living color."

"Pleased to meet you, I'm Gerry and this is my friend Pete," said Williams shaking the restaurant owner's hand.

"Nice to meet you too and as I said if you need anything just holler." Al said starting to make his way back to the bar.

Shelby whispered, "Good, I'm glad we cleared the air with him."

"Yes, I know what you mean," Williams agreed.

Al was still wary of the two men playing pool in his restaurant. Something wasn't right. These guys were both strikingly good looking, in tremendous shape and seemed to be very personable. Al wondered who they could be, but was coming up blank.

A short while after, two young men came striding into the restaurant and headed straight to the back where Williams and Shelby were playing pool. One of them asked if they wanted to have a game of doubles, for ten dollars a game and before they could answer, had inserted some coins into one of the other tables and was racking the balls. Williams and Shelby got into some small talk with the young men and found out they were from a small town to the south of there and were seasonal workers. One of them said they hadn't seen Williams and Shelby there before. Williams replied that they were passing through on their way to visit some of his relatives in Seattle. This seemed to be a good reason to explain what they were doing there.

The young men accepted this, one of them saying, "I guess you're not in any big hurry to get there?"

"Well, we are and we aren't," muttered Williams. "It will be nice to see relatives I haven't seen for quite awhile but we don't want to impose on them for very long."
Not fully understanding what Williams meant, the young men began to talk about how close the games had been. They were obviously pool sharks and after having beaten Williams and Shelby three times in a row, said they had to go. Williams paid them their winnings and they left.

\* \* \* \*

At the noon conference call, chaired by Base Commander Maty, the technical director from the missile manufacturing plant told everyone on the call that they had successfully simulated the reset of the detonation counter to its maximum value, without causing the warheads to detonate and engineers had already been dispatched to reset the counter in the missile. Base Commander Maty asked him what time they would be arriving and was told around three o'clock. The base commander was concerned that this would only give them an hour to work on the missile once they arrived, but was reassured that the change wouldn't take long. The commander reluctantly accepted this and ended the call.

Following the call, Base Commander Maty met with his officers and was extremely pleased to hear about the cooperation they were getting from the base commander at Edwards Air Force base, in California. He had agreed to accommodate all their B-52's and C-5's and most of them were already in the air on their way. He thought to himself this was the United States military at its finest. It always upset him when he heard the military being criticized. If people could only realize it was because of them that the United States was the most powerful country in the world.

\*    \*    \*    \*

Just after noon on Monday afternoon, Major Trsenkov arrived in Cold Water Falls and met up with the agents who had been trailing the Americans all night. The trip west had gone very well for him because there had apparently been blizzard-like conditions south of the border, but the weather in Canada had been clear. Sam had driven along the trans-Canada highway at speeds over one hundred miles an hour and had made excellent time. At a British Columbia-Montana border crossing, an hour or so earlier, nobody had paid any attention to the dark Lincoln with Ontario plates as they entered into the United States.

\*    \*    \*    \*

At a very brief conference call Monday afternoon, Base Commander Maty told Deputy Secretary of Defence

Craig and senior officials from the Pentagon that a way had been found to postpone the detonation of the warheads. They were obviously all very pleased to hear this news, but like the base commander, concerned that the engineers doing the resetting wouldn't be arriving at the base for another hour.

\*   \*   \*   \*

Around two-thirty Monday afternoon, the Soviet informant in the Minot police department phoned the farm to let them know there was a rumour that the Americans had found a way to stop the missile from exploding. The agents at the farm said they would pass the information along and immediately communicated the information to Major Trsenkov.

\*   \*   \*   \*

Just before three o'clock, Base Commander Maty drove out to the main airstrip and waited for the missile manufacturer's engineers to arrive. They touched down in an old Huron turboprop and taxied over to the hangar area where the base commander was waiting. Once the aircraft came to a stop, he drove and parked below its cargo door and waited for the passenger stairs to be lowered. Although the majority of his officers knew about the crisis, by picking up the engineers himself he was avoiding having to explain their mission to anyone else. He greeted them as they stepped down off the plane and asked them to get into his Jeep. It was only just big enough for the four of them and all their equipment. Luckily, three of them had slight builds which allowed them to squeeze into the back. The base commander told them he realized the Jeep wasn't very comfortable, but said it wouldn't take them long to get to the damaged silo. He said he hoped that whatever they had to do wouldn't take long. The engineer sitting in the front said that as long as the damaged electronics rack back plane connectors had been replaced, which he said he understood to be the case, it would only take a few minutes to make the change. Each of the engineers was carrying a large metal case and the base commander asked them what was in them. One of the engineers sitting in the back said they had each brought a complete air data computer unit and diagnostics equipment with them, in case a complete unit or any replacement parts were needed.

"Good" said the base commander. "I like people who plan ahead, especially in a situation like this, where we could all be blown to kingdom come in less than an hour from now."

As soon as they reached the silo, the base commander asked everyone inside to leave, regardless of what they were doing. He told them engineers were there to make modifications to the missile's electronics systems. As the base commander was leaving the silo, he gave one of the engineers a phone number and asked him to call him the instant the counter had been successfully reset.

Base Commander Maty drove to the nearest launch control facility, where the operators were most surprised to see him. He told them he was conducting a routine check. They found this to be most unusual because normally his senior officers accompanied him when he conducted inspections. Although feeling distracted by the real issue, he listened briefly to their comments about the day-to-day operation of the facility. Their comments were all fairly benign, from they were still waiting for some small warning light bulbs to be replaced, to the need for a new coffee maker. It was three twenty-two when he sat down at the console closest to an air raid siren activation button and waited for the phone to ring. As he sat there, drinking a coffee from a vending machine, he watched the second hand ticking on the large clock on the wall.

While the base commander waited, he conjectured about what would happen if he did actually have to sound the air raid siren. He knew the main concentrations of personnel were either in the headquarters buildings or around the hangers, next to the main airstrip and that there were underground fallout shelters under each of the areas. Operational personnel in the underground launch control facilities should be safe and knew not to leave their stations. It was the personnel in transit at the time of the explosion that would be most vulnerable. Impromptu air raid drills were conducted twice a year, so everyone on the base should know exactly where to go when the siren sounded. It was planned that he would be meeting his wife and boys in the fallout shelter under the base headquarters building, where he had an office and accommodations for him and his family. He was confident that if there was an explosion, it would only be a matter of time until everyone below ground would be rescued safely. He had total faith in the United States military's commitment to those in its employment. He knew that military personnel would always come first in the time of conflict. After all, they were the defenders of all the people and without them, the people and country would perish.

Once everyone had left the silo, the engineers from the missile manufacturer set up their equipment. The now-nervous engineers saw that the electronics rack back plane connectors had already been replaced. They attached a small programming device to one of the connectors. After monitoring instruction execution for several minutes, one of the engineers, his hands shaking, entered the command string to reset the detonation countdown variable. No ill effects to the missile's electronic systems were observed and the engineers congratulated each other. The modification had gained them three more days to try and come up with a permanent fix. If they got close to the next detonation countdown deadline, the counter could be reset again. One of the engineers climbed up to the top level of the silo and phoned the base commander with the good news. It was three twenty-eight.

"Great news!" said the base commander. "Great job! I'll come and pick you up."

Following the call, the base commander, much perkier now the immediate crisis had been averted, said his goodbyes to the launch control operators and left the facility.

*   *   *   *

Al could see the two strangers watching TV at the back of the bar, as his happy hour regulars started to come in. He walked back to where the strangers were sitting and asked if he could get them anything.

"I could use something to eat; it seems like hours since I ate," said Shelby.

"How about a burger and fries?" asked Al.

"Yes, me too," said Williams.

"Two burgers and fries coming right up," said Al, carrying some empty beer bottles back to the bar.

It was just after four and another afternoon talk show had just begun, there were no news bulletins yet. Williams and Shelby ate the burgers and fries and decided they would wait for the six o'clock evening news. They played some more pool and watched a sports talk show to pass the time.

\*    \*    \*    \*

Major Trsenkov, parked on the main street of Cold Water Falls, was tuned to an all-news radio station. It was now four-thirty and there was no news about an explosion, so it seemed the rumour about them finding a way to stop the detonation had been true. He walked down the street until he found a payphone and phoned General Tsoff using an international calling card. When he got through to the general, he just said, "Explosion stopped," and hung up. He hated speaking with the general like this, but it wasn't a secure phone line.

\*    \*    \*    \*

In Al's restaurant, six o'clock arrived and at the top of the news there was no mention of an explosion.

"They must have found a way to stop it," whispered Shelby.

"But how?" whispered Williams. "Stopping the detonation countdown should have caused the warheads to immediately explode."

While Williams and Shelby were watching the news, Alan Ascot, the owner of Al's, was in his office behind the bar, whispering into the phone.

"Could I speak to Dick please?" he said quietly.

Al was told that Dick Farley, the Cold Water Falls police chief, had already left for the day.

Al asked for the Chief's home number and was told it couldn't be given out.

"Who am I speaking to?" asked Al.

He was told it was the evening shift supervisor.

"I just wanted to let him know that two strangers have been in my restaurant all day. They haven't caused any trouble, but I just heard on the radio that two escaped convicts are on the run," said Al quietly.

After providing his name and phone number, he was thanked for the information. The shift supervisor didn't really want to bother the chief at his home, although it seemed as though this guy knew him. He decided he would let him know about the call in the morning, because he hadn't heard anything about the two escaped convicts.

As soon as the news finished, Williams paid the bill and he and Shelby left the restaurant.

\*   \*   \*   \*

Major Trsenkov and his agents saw the Americans come out of the restaurant. After taking a few minutes to warm up their old truck, they drove off in a westerly direction, unaware that they were being followed as they left Cold Water Falls early on that Monday evening. After about an hour or so, they came to a small town called Liberty and Williams suggested to Shelby that they find a place to stay so they could get some sleep. Sure enough, it wasn't too long until they found a motel.

They put the TV on as soon as they got into their room at the Spruce Motel; there were still no news bulletins, just the usual nightly sitcoms. The explosion obviously hadn't happened there was no way to cover it up.

"They must have found a way to stop it, but how?" said Williams.

"Let's talk about it in the morning," said Shelby, yawning.

"Anyway, I'm still confident we can escape," yawned Williams.

Shelby was already snoring and Williams soon joined him.

# CHAPTER 6

### Tuesday February 16

Shelby was woken out of a deep sleep by bright lights shining on the wall of the motel room. He peeked out from behind the curtains and saw a police car.

He woke Williams saying, "You need to get up! It looks like the cops might be on to us. They're outside, checking license plates."

"What time is it?" Williams asked, yawning.

Shelby checked his watch. "Three fifteen."

"We'd better get out of here!" said Williams, quickly getting dressed.

Not seeing anything moving outside, they got into their snow-covered truck and headed out of the motel parking lot, driving past a police car parked outside the motel office. They could see two police officers in conversation with someone behind the counter. Once they got out on the highway, Williams checked the rear view mirror and saw that no one was following them.

"Do you think they're on to us?" asked Shelby.

"Who knows?" Williams reached back, opened his backpack, took out the stamina pills bottle and offered it to Shelby. Shelby took two pills, swallowed them and handed the bottle back to Williams who took three pills out of the bottle, swallowed them and put the bottle back in his backpack.

"These things are great; I don't think we'd have got this far without them."

This was the first time Williams and Shelby had come anywhere close to getting caught by the police - as far as they knew.

\*    \*    \*    \*

Major Trsenkov and his agents, after following the Americans to the motel, had spent the night in a diner along the highway close to the motel. After seeing the Americans leave the motel, they began to follow them again.

\*    \*    \*    \*

As they travelled west, Williams apologized to Shelby for not being able, in General Tsoff's words, "...fully execute the mission as planned." They had traveled for about twenty miles, Williams continuing to rehash the events of the last few days, when bright headlights appeared right behind them and they heard what sounded like gunfire. The truck's rear window shattered just as Shelby was turning to see what was happening behind them. Automatic gunfire lit up the morning darkness.

"I guess the general's men have caught up with us too!" said Williams.

"Looks like it," said Shelby.

"I told you not to open fire!" shouted Major Trsenkov, trying to grab an automatic weapon. "Now they know we've found them."

Williams told Shelby to get the pistol out of his backpack. Williams could see that the dark vehicle behind them no longer had its headlights on and thought, *Two can play at this game* and turned his lights off. It was now difficult for both drivers to see ahead of them. There were no tail lights for Sam to follow and it was difficult for Williams to see the road ahead, but gradually their eyes adjusted.

"Sam, pull up beside the truck. We need to kill them now! This is the perfect time and place," said the major. Sam accelerated and moved up alongside the old truck, but almost immediately had to brake and pull in behind it again when he saw approaching headlights.

"What are you doing?" asked the major somewhat agitated.

"There was a car coming towards us," said Sam nervously.

The car passed and Sam came up alongside the truck again. Looking out of the driver's side window, Williams could see what looked like an automatic weapon beginning to protrude out of the passenger side front window of the car, now alongside him. He fired off a round of bullets at the car and they ricocheted off its hood and roof, making loud metallic popping sounds. The car braked and disappeared out of sight.

The major told Ivan , sitting next to him in the backseat, to try and shoot them from behind and automatic gunfire lit up the darkness once again.

Williams shouted, "Here!" giving the pistol to Shelby "Return fire. There are more ammunition clips in the backpack."

Shelby quickly reloaded the pistol and shot at the dark car behind, through the truck's smashed back window.

The major told Anton to start shooting as well and Anton readied his automatic weapon as Sam came right up behind the truck. Both automatic weapons started firing into the back of truck's cab. Both Ivan and Anton were firing out of the front passenger side window. Shelby exchanged fire as best he could while ducking behind the bench seat, while bullets were thudding into the back of it. A bullet smashed into the dashboard, just missing Williams and he pressed down as hard as he could on the accelerator pedal, but the truck wouldn't go any faster. Shots continued to ricochet around inside the truck's cab.

Williams said, "This truck won't go any faster, so let's see how good its brakes are. Brace yourself."

Shelby held onto the dashboard with both hands, as Williams put both feet down on the brake pedal. Almost instantly, there was a loud metal-on-metal crunching sound and a strong smell of burning rubber.

Upon impact, Anton had dropped his automatic weapon out of the passenger side window and banged his head on the windshield. Next to him, Sam's chest had been crushed by the steering wheel and both of their heads were drooping forward. Through the rear view mirror, Williams could see that the vehicle behind them was engulfed in billowing steam, its hazard lights flashing.

Neither Williams nor Shelby had been hurt on impact. Williams managed to untangle the truck from the wreckage and turning the headlights back on, slowly drove off into the pitch black night.

Shelby let out a sigh. "Can you believe this? Less than forty eight hours ago these people were our friends, doing all they could for us and now they're trying to kill us?"

"Things change quickly in this business, especially when things go wrong. Life is cheap to these people, particularly the lives of Americans, we've been their enemies for decades," said Williams.

"You would think they'd cut us some slack after what we've done for them!"

"They don't care. As we discussed, if we'd gone back to Moscow, they would have likely killed us. At least now we're in control of our own destiny."

"Yes, I guess you're right. You know, this whole thing has been totally crazy. I go on vacation and end up in the Soviet Air Force and a key member of one of the most important missions in their history. It's been like a bad dream," Shelby said.

Williams asked him if he could hear a scraping noise and still smell burning rubber. Shelby said he could.

*   *   *   *

Sam and Anton appeared to be dead. Major Trsenkov had banged his head on the seat in front and was bleeding slightly from his forehead. Ivan, sitting in the back seat beside the major, was rubbing his neck and cursing loudly. They could feel the heat from the scalding hot steam from the cracked radiator coming in through the shattered windshield. The major tried to open his door but it wouldn't budge. He asked Ivan if he could open his and Ivan said he couldn't. They could see lights outside and someone was banging on Ivan's window. Ivan tried to lower it, but it wouldn't move. Someone shouted in through the windshield that they were going to smash the back window, so they should cover their faces. Ivan's window shattered just as he was putting his hands up to protect his face. Someone peered in and enquired how badly they were hurt.

The major said, "Check those in the front first. They are hurt far worse than us and may even be dead."

The major and Ivan were told to get out the car as quickly as they could because it could catch fire at any moment. Ivan said that all the glass needed to be removed from the smashed window before they could get out and asked for the tire jack that had been used to smash it. With great difficulty, Ivan and the major squeezed out through the shattered back window. By then there were a number of vehicles and people surrounding the wrecked Lincoln, most of them asking what had happened. The major collected himself and calmly said he thought they had hit an animal and it must have run off. Some people were holding shell casings and others were pointing at an automatic weapon lying by the side of the road. Without explanation, the major picked up the weapon and asked those with shell casings to give them to him. He then asked if someone could give them a ride to the nearest town so they could call the police. Although reluctant to allow them to leave the scene of the accident, the person who had smashed the window agreed to give them a ride.

When they came to a gas station on the outskirts of Liberty, Major Trsenkov asked the driver to stop next to a payphone. He called the farm, told them what had happened and asked them to arrange for local agents to pick him and Ivan up. He did his best to tell them where they were currently located. He went back to the vehicle and told the driver that the police were on their way. He asked the driver how he took his coffee and motioned to Ivan to get out of the car. The two of them headed towards the gas station building. As they were walking, the major told Ivan that they were not going back to the scene of the accident, but would be staying there until they were picked up.

They entered the gas station office and the major told the mechanic, the only person there, that someone was coming to pick them up and asked if it was alright if they waited there. The mechanic, somewhat confused, said that it was not a problem and asked what the guy in the car was waiting for. The major said he didn't know and the mechanic went out to the car. He came back and said the person in the car was waiting for them to bring him a coffee. The major waved the automatic weapon, which had been concealed under his coat, at the mechanic and told him to stand facing the wall of the office. He told Ivan to go and tell the driver to come and get his own coffee. The driver came into the gas station office complaining about why he had to get his own coffee and the major pointed the automatic weapon at him. He told him to shut up and go and stand next to the mechanic, facing the wall.

*   *   *   *

Once Williams could see that they weren't being followed, he pulled over to the side of the road, jumped out and went to look at the back of the truck. One of the tail lights was smashed and he could see that the truck's box had shifted off its frame and was sloping down to one side. The underside of the box was touching on one of the back tires. He called to Shelby to come and help him. They pushed the box back up onto the truck's frame as best they could, so it was no longer touching the tire.

"I think that should do it," said Williams.

"Let's get out of here then," said Shelby. "We just came very close to getting killed back there!"

"You know," said Williams, "I don't think the police are on to us yet, but it seems the major and his men definitely are."

"You're not kidding!" said Shelby. "I saw my life flash right before my eyes, just now."

It was almost five in the morning and still very dark as they drove off.

"I think we should head for Spokane," said Williams. "It will be much harder for anyone to find us in a big city."

Driving west they hadn't seen an open gas station and the truck was almost out of gas. Williams had decided that whenever he did find one open, he would buy some gas cans, so that at least they would have a reserve from now on.

\*   \*   \*   \*

Major Trsenkov was sitting in the gas station office, pointing his weapon at the mechanic and the driver. Ivan was leaning in the doorway, smoking a cigarette, when they saw a car pull up to the pumps. The major told Ivan to go and serve them. Ivan put his cigarette out and walked out to the pumps. The car had out of state plates, so the driver didn't find anything strange about Ivan pumping his gas. Ivan returned to the office and plonked a twenty dollar bill down on the counter. The major looked at his watch and wondered how long it was going to be until they were picked up. Ten minutes later, a black sedan pulled up in front of the gas station building. The major told Ivan to go and get in the car and turned his attention to the hostages.

"Gentlemen, through no fault of your own, you have become mixed up in this. I ask that you tell no one about any of this or I guarantee you will both be hunted down and killed like dogs. Do you understand?"

They both nodded nervously still facing the wall.

When they heard the car pull away, the driver and mechanic, still very scared, began to discuss what they should do.

"I think we should just forget this ever happened, as we have just been requested to," said the mechanic.

"You really think so?" said the driver.

"Yes. Don't you think he meant what he said? If we contact the police, they will kill us and they obviously know where to find me. I would really appreciate it if you would forget it ever happened. It will likely be harder for them to find you, but I have no doubt they will. How did you come to be with them anyway?" asked the mechanic.

"They were involved in an accident west of here, on Highway 2. The guy with the gun said they hit an animal and it had run off, but there was an automatic weapon and numerous shell casings in the road. Their car was badly damaged and it looked like the driver and the passenger in the front seat may have died in the accident. They asked someone to help them find a telephone, so they could call the police and I believed them, even though I was suspicious because of the weapon and their foreign accents."

"So I don't need to tell you to keep your mouth shut! You should already know that after what you've just told me," said the mechanic.

"Yes, you're right. I was on my way to work this morning and I haven't had a chance to call in yet to say I'll be late. Can I use your phone?"

"Sure go ahead, but please let someone else worry about catching up with these people. I certainly don't want to die," the mechanic said.

"Don't worry, I'm with you."

"I hope there weren't too many people at the scene of the accident or you may have some explaining to do to the police. Anyway, I'm sure you'll have a good story ready, like you dropped them off and went to work. Please don't mention me. You know there's another service station just up the road and there's a phone there too. Just say you dropped them off there," said the mechanic.

"Thanks. I'll check it out. Don't worry - if anyone contacts me, I won't mention you."

The mechanic waited until the driver had phoned his work and driven off, then went back to the oil change he was doing when he had been interrupted.

\*   \*   \*   \*

Now back on the road heading west, Major Trsenkov figured they were several hours behind the Americans. They soon got back to the scene of the accident and as they sped by, could see several highway patrol cars, a fire truck and two ambulances. The wrecked Lincoln was off to the side of the road behind a tow truck. There was a Medivac helicopter there too, so the major thought perhaps there was hope for Sam and Anton - maybe they hadn't been fatally injured after all. The major didn't give the scene a second thought once they had passed by, understanding it was just part of the job. His only interest once again, was to catch up to the Americans and kill them. He wondered where they might be heading.

* * * *

Williams and Shelby got lucky and found a gas station just opening up. Williams pulled up to the pumps and a young mechanic, wiping the grease from his hands, came out to help them. Williams asked him if he had any gas cans he could buy. The mechanic said he didn't think so, but he'd check. Williams asked him how far it was to Spokane from here and which was the best way to get there. The mechanic told him to stay on Highway 2 and then take Interstate 95 south and Interstate 90 west. He said he figured it was just over two hundred miles and it would take them, three to four hours to get there. After gassing up the truck the young mechanic found an old gas can, filled it up and placed in the back of the truck. Williams paid him and thanked him for his help.

They pulled out of the gas station and continued to head west. Fifteen minutes into Idaho they were traveling south on I 95, past a sign indicating that Spokane was one hundred and ninety five miles ahead. Williams was pushing the truck as hard as he could, but it was still only going just over sixty miles an hour. They were driving through blowing snow again and finding some of the lanes on the interstate closed. Williams figured they should find a motel and lie low once they got to Spokane, making it almost impossible to track them down.

\*   \*   \*   \*

At a Tuesday morning conference call, SAC Chief of Staff Callaghan told Base Commander Maty that the permanent solution for the compromised missile was to remove the complete nosecone containing the nuclear warheads, then fly it out and ditch it in the Pacific Ocean. Scientists from the Department of Energy had apparently already looked into exploding the warheads in the desert but had rejected this because it would be observed by too many people living in nearby communities and would lead to too many questions. An underwater explosion in waters deep enough to cover Mount Everest seemed to be by far the best option. The scientists said that although there would be a significant spray dome, it should dissipate very rapidly, leaving no trace of the explosion. The water displaced would be radioactive, but the particles would start to break up almost immediately. They had put the Pacific Tsunami Warning Center in Honolulu on alert and would be alerting the United States Air Force weather stations on Midway and Wake Islands also. Callaghan told the base commander that information about the incident at Minot had been relayed to all the other missile bases in the United States and they were all on high alert. Also, the President had informed the Prime Minister in England and he had put all the missiles sites over there on heightened alert also.

Callaghan informed the base commander that the President had been briefed and although he had a few concerns, had approved the plan to ditch the nosecone in the Pacific Ocean. He said that the President was very pleased to see how well contained everything had been so far, which, besides stopping the detonation and finding those responsible was his highest priority.

\*    \*    \*    \*

At Warren Air Force Base near Cheyenne, Wyoming, the base commander had been informed by SAC that his ICBM Emplacer-Extractor, currently being used to replace Minutemen with Peacekeeper missiles, was needed at Minot Air Force base as soon as possible. He was ordered to have his men work around the clock to dismantle it and have it ready to be transported to Minot. Cranes were already lifting the large steel structures onto flatbed railway cars, their high booms swinging backwards and forwards. Trucks with banks of floodlights in the back were lighting up the whole area. It was estimated that within the next five to six hours, the train should be ready to begin its journey to Minot, North Dakota. Some of the flatbed railcars carrying parts of the ICBM Emplacer-Extractor were already covered with tarpaulins, with the stamp of the United States Air Force visible. The military train was going to be given priority over regular freight trains, but not over passenger trains, they didn't want any undue attention drawn to it. It would be taking the main northerly rail line through the western parts of the states of Nebraska, South and North Dakota.

\*    \*    \*    \*

Williams had changed his mind about finding a motel and suggested they ditch the truck and hop a westbound freight. Shelby was surprised at this but agreed. The idea of heading for Australia had come to Williams a few miles back, while they were sitting at a railway crossing, waiting for a passenger train to speed by. He put this to Shelby, who said he guessed they had to go somewhere to get away and that sure would be getting away. Williams said he figured they could hang out with his sister and her husband for a while. Shelby became quite excited about the idea and asked Williams if he really thought they could make it there. Why not said Williams I've wanted to go there to visit my sister since she moved down there a few years back.

Williams found a trail leading down to the railway tracks and drove into some snow-covered bushes to hide the truck. After about half an hour, they could see the bright headlight of a train off in the distance. It turned out to be a freight train with a variety of container railcars. As it was approaching, it seemed to be going quite slow, but as it began to pass by them, they realized it was actually going quite fast and they needed to be running at the same speed as the train to stand any chance of getting on board. There were only a few cars left by the time they got up the needed speed. Williams managed to scramble up onto a container car and helped Shelby get on board. It was most uncomfortable. There was a lot of vibration and the railcar they were on was coated in ice. They moved to the next railcar which seemed less icy and offered more shelter from the bitterly cold wind. The railcars were screeching loudly as they maneuvered around the curves along the track. Williams was thinking "iron horse" was a good name, because it felt like you were riding one. They wished they had purchased gloves and jackets with hoods back in Cold Water Falls, because their hands and ears were already freezing cold. They were trying to warm their hands by keeping them in their pockets, but had no way of warming their ears. Shelby suggested they tie their socks together and loop them around their heads, over their ears, but Williams rejected this idea saying their feet would freeze. The only option they had was to keep taking their hands out of their pockets and putting them over their ears. Shelby's ears hurt so much that he took his jacket off and used it to cover his head. Williams did the same thing, worrying that his ears might be getting frostbitten. They had frozen snow in their hair and their faces were turning reddish blue. Shelby couldn't stop his teeth from chattering and his nose hurt if he breathed in too quickly. Williams suggested they jump up and down to try and get warm. They tried it, but their bodies ached so much from the cold that they were unable to do it for very long. Besides, standing up also exposed them to the cold wind.

"Think warm thoughts," said Williams. "Pretend you're sitting on the beach on a tropical island somewhere."

Shelby said, "I've got an idea. Why don't we hug each other?"

"You know, that's not a bad idea. I'm willing to try anything."

They looked like fully-clothed wrestlers, their hands tucked into each other's sleeves, each having the other in a headlock. The train continued on its journey as the men huddled together, both soon falling asleep.

A number of hours later they awoke as numerous railway tracks and railcars were coming into view on either side of them. They had arrived in the port of Seattle.

As the train began to slow down, the two men jumped off and began to explore their new surroundings. They found a boxcar in one of the sidings that was unlocked and as soon as they got inside started to feel warmer almost immediately. Although there was no heat inside the boxcar, it felt warm just to be out of the wind. Within an hour or so they were feeling much better, now that they were sheltered, rather than outside directly exposed to the elements.

\*     \*     \*     \*

Base Commander Maty began a Tuesday afternoon conference call with the FBI, state and local police authorities with an apology for not being able to meet with them before now. He explained that since very early the previous morning, he had been focusing all his attention on stopping the potential detonation of the missile in the damaged silo. On the call were Ken Harris, Deputy Director of the Federal Bureau of Investigation; several of his senior federal agents; Minot Police Chief Grogan; Director McNally of the North Dakota State Police; and a number of other high ranking state and local police officials. The base commander said he understood that the FBI would be providing backup support to the state and local police authorities, even though this was not officially an inter-state matter.

He asked Minot Police Chief Grogan if he had made any progress in apprehending those responsible for the break-in. Grogan said there had been an incident at the border early on Sunday morning and that on Sunday afternoon, a warrant had been obtained for the arrest of two men staying at the Elk Motel, close to the border. The men were suspected of crashing the border. But when troopers went to serve the warrant, the men had already left the motel. The previous day he had been contacted by the Tollesbury police about a statement from someone who had been forced to drive a paratrooper from the north side of the base up to Ebdon ski resort on Saturday afternoon.

"That's interesting because a group of local people came to the base on Saturday afternoon, saying they were looking for one of their friends. He may have been the one who was forced to drive the paratrooper up to the ski resort," said Base Commander Maty. Then he asked Director McNally if he had anything to add. He said he was aware of the incidents at the border crossing, Elk Motel and the ski resort but didn't have anything else to add.

Base Commander Maty then asked Deputy Director Harris if he would chair the remainder of that meeting and future meetings. Harris said he would and also said that as of that morning, this had become an FBI case. He informed the others that information had been received from the police in Cold Water Falls, Montana, that they had received a call the previous day about two strangers who had spent most of the day in a local restaurant there. They were also checking on another incident early that morning, west of the town of Liberty, Montana. A vehicle with province of Ontario license plates was involved in a serious accident. According to witnesses, an automatic weapon and shell casings were found at the scene and two of the occupants who were in the badly damaged vehicle quickly left the scene of the accident. Two other occupants in the vehicle were fatally injured. There are suspicions that the two suspects may have been involved in the accident, because the timeline fits. He said that the police were following up on both of these leads and would provide further information on them as it became available.

"Thank you," said the base commander. "As I mentioned at the outset of the meeting, I am sorry that this is the first time we have been able to get together. I suggest we meet again tomorrow at the same time, to discuss our progress." He ended the call.

\* \* \* \*

After scouring the city of Spokane for several hours, Soviet agents located the Americans' pickup truck. Based on where they'd found it, Major Trsenkov figured the Americans must have hopped a train. He found a payphone and phoned an agent in Seattle and asked where trains go upon entering the city. He was told that most passenger trains normally terminate their journeys at the main downtown train station, and container freights usually terminate their journeys in the port of Seattle. All other freight trains get routed to different industrial areas via a central hub, north-east of the city. Even though it was very unlikely the Americans would have managed to climb aboard a passenger train, the major requested agents be sent to all three locations. After he got off the phone with the agent from Seattle, he phoned General Tsoff.

When one of the general's regular telephones rang, he stood up, reached over and picked it up. Major Trsenkov informed him they had lost the Americans and because it was not a secure line, hung up immediately. The general, who was already quite despondent that the mission had failed and that the Americans were being hunted down to be killed, suddenly felt very faint and collapsed to the floor of his office. It was snowing lightly in Moscow that night and sixty-four-year-old General Vladimir Tsoff of the Strategic Rocket Wing of the Soviet Department of Defense was dead.

\*　　\*　　\*　　\*

Williams and Shelby waited until dusk before leaving the boxcar to look around the port area. Huge container ships, most of them almost as long as a football field, were well lit and they were able to determine that there were at least a dozen of them in the port, all in different stages of being unloaded or loaded. There were groups of men everywhere on the dockside and they were careful not to let anyone see them. They had seen enough for now and made their way back to the relative safety of the boxcar under the cover of darkness.

\*　　\*　　\*　　\*

Base Commander Maty hadn't slept for almost two days since first being informed about the potential nuclear explosion and was totally exhausted. He asked Lieutenant Colonel Smith to take over command while he went to get some sleep. His wife was surprised to see him as he came through the front door and asked him if he wanted anything to eat. He said he was too tired to eat and just wanted to go to bed. His wife followed him up the stairs and helped him get undressed and into bed. Although he was extremely tired, sleep wouldn't come. He couldn't stop going over the events of the last two days. The whole situation seemed so unreal. How could this have happened here at Minot? He couldn't stop thinking about who could have done it. He wouldn't have thought many people knew how to trigger the detonation countdown of a nuclear warhead! He was starting to run through the possibilities, when sleep finally overcame him.

Suddenly, outside the bedroom window, there was the deafening sound of a huge explosion and blinding flashes of white light, which turned night into day. The curtains, blinds and furniture were all swept against the far wall. The air was thick with dust and debris and a mushroom cloud could be clearly seen, forming high up in the night sky. A massive crater slowly came into view as the smoke began to clear. Fires were burning everywhere.

The base commander awoke, sweating profusely. He jumped out of bed, ran over and looked out of the bedroom window. Outside it was dark, with a few dim lights visible off in the distance. His wife burst into the bedroom and asked him if everything was alright.

He turned towards her and said, "Yes, everything's alright. I was just having a nightmare about the end of the world - nothing too serious."

His wife helped him get back into bed and told him he had only been asleep for about an hour. He fell back to sleep instantly.

# CHAPTER 7

### Wednesday February 17

Williams and Shelby awoke early on Wednesday morning feeling really hungry, but there wasn't much they could do about it. They dry shaved using a razor Shelby had brought with him to the ski resort. Although their hair was greasy and their clothes soiled, they both looked reasonably presentable. Upon leaving the boxcar, they could see huge cranes and gantries loading a monstrous ship with containers from the train that they had arrived on yesterday. The containers were multi-coloured, with large, meaningless letters like CSL, APL and POL painted on them.

As they approached a gang of men on the dockside, a tough-looking dock worker greeted them saying, "Good day."

"We're looking for passage across the Pacific and we're willing to pay top dollar and work if need be," said Williams.

In a very deep voice, the dock worker told them that these were box ships that didn't take passengers. He suggested they go and check with the passenger shipping lines, located near the port entrance.

"We're working men, not tourists and would feel much more at home on one of these ships," insisted Williams.

The dock worker figured Williams wasn't going to take no for an answer and said he would take them to meet one of the container ship skippers.

*    *    *    *

Following the nightmare, Base Commander Maty had slept well and the following morning, after eating a home-cooked breakfast, headed back over to the base headquarters building. It was a bright sunny morning and he felt refreshed after having had a good night's sleep.

He chaired a very brief ten o'clock conference call with SAC and told everyone on the call that the train carrying the ICBM Emplacer-Extractor extractor tripod should be arriving at the base that night. He said that was all the new news he had to report at the moment and he ended the call.

At an even briefer conference call with the FBI and different police authorities that afternoon, FBI Director Harris said he didn't have anything new to report and that call also ended quickly.

* * * *

Dusk was rapidly approaching as one of the last containers was being lowered into place on the massive container ship. It would be another four hours before the ship would be slowly towed out into Puget Sound and make its way through the Sound's straits, channels and narrows to the Pacific. Williams had paid handsomely for the one-way trip to Singapore and had agreed that he and Shelby would stay out of the way. Although initially reluctant to allow them aboard, once Williams had offered him five thousand dollars cash, the captain had quickly agreed to take them. The captain told the crew that Williams and Shelby were industrial financiers, representing the interests of the shipping line's major shareholders. This was a bit of a stretch, given the way they looked, but the crew seemed to have accepted the explanation. They were on board the *Asian Trader*, a container transporting ship, operated out of the port of Hong Kong. The ship was carrying hundreds of containers, all stacked high in rows on the main deck. There was a multi-storey superstructure at the stern of the ship which looked like one of the numerous white apartment complexes you see along the beaches in Florida. This structure took up less than ten percent of the space on the ship; the remaining ninety percent was completely filled with containers. All the way up the side of the accommodation block were catwalks. They jutted out like balconies, each one enclosed with high railings. Hanging off the side of the accommodation block were two impressive looking lifeboats, one larger than the other, both orange.

Williams and Shelby were given a tour of the ship by the communications officer, Hugh. They climbed up to the top floor of the accommodation block and were taken down a passageway onto the bridge. It overlooked the containers. They were told the ship was over three hundred metres in length, but all they knew was it seemed to be an incredible distance from where they were standing to the bow of the ship. The captain welcomed them to the bridge and told them that once the ship's manifest had been reviewed, they would be on their way. He seemed excited to have them on board and took great pride in showing them the ships navigational instruments. Williams and Shelby tried their best to show genuine interest, as he showed them barometers, barographs, radar screens, chronometers, compasses and all kinds of other instruments. He described in detail what each one of them was for – measuring atmospheric pressure, calculating wind speed, determining the ship's position, speed and heading. They could tell by the enthusiasm he showed when describing each one of them that this was his playground. There were microphones, numerous telephones and what looked like old fashioned walkie-talkies everywhere. There was a large display panel on the wall, showing the entire layout of the ship. Small lights were lit up on the display, all of them green. These apparently alerted the crew to fire or water problems anywhere on the ship. He introduced them to some of his officers and the helmsman, who were reviewing a large chart. He jokingly told them the ship pretty much steered itself, while poking the helmsman in the ribs. He said it stayed on course by itself once it entered the major east-west shipping lanes. He said the tricky part was navigating in and out of harbors. He told them a pilot would soon be coming aboard to assist them to manoeuvre the ship up through Puget Sound. Away from his officers, he told them they were lucky to be on his ship, because his crew was from Hong Kong and they all spoke good English. He said most of the other container ships in the port were from Shenzhen or Shanghai and the crews on those ships spoke very little English. One of the telephones on the bridge rang and the captain politely excused himself.

This was Williams and Shelby's chance to leave the bridge. Hugh took them down to the "communal floor", as he described it. They were shown the galley, which was very clean and the crew lounge, which was very well furnished. They were surprised to find a movie theatre, swimming pool, sauna and hot tub on board. There was also a recreation room with a table tennis table and pool tables. They were not shown the captain's quarters, which was on the same floor, but were told he had an office, bedroom and his own bathroom.

Just as they were completing the tour, an officer handed them some keys and asked Hugh to show them where their cabins were. Their cabins were quite small and everything was bolted down. They had a window, not a porthole, a wall sink and toilet, which gave the cabin the look of a prison cell. There was a bed attached to the wall and Hugh told them there were communal showers and washrooms on each floor.

*You don't get much of a room on a container ship for five hundred dollars a day*, thought Williams.

\*   \*   \*   \*

As he sat in his sparsely furnished office in the base headquarters building, Base Commander Maty was thinking about the lack of progress being made by the FBI-supported police authorities. Never having worked with the FBI before, he hadn't realized how dependent they were on the state and local police authorities. Essentially all they were doing was providing information whenever it became available. From what he could tell, the FBI was best suited for long-term surveillance and evidence collection, on major criminal activities. They did not seem to be well suited for situations that required immediate action. Anyway, it was only a few days after the infiltration and these things probably took time, so he would cut them some slack.

\*   \*   \*   \*

The train carrying the ICBM Emplacer-Extractor had arrived at Minot Air Force base and cranes were already beginning to load large sections on to flatbed trucks. It had been years since there had been so much excitement on the base. People were constantly arriving and a makeshift parking lot had been set up close to the damaged silo. The engineers from the missile manufacturer who had reset the detonation countdown variable were still on the base and would be staying until the nosecone had been detached and was on its way to be ditched. Engineers from the silo manufacturer were working on repairing the main missile cover hydraulics control system. A number of local contractors had been brought in to provide the required scaffolding and floodlighting around and above the damaged silo. It was a hive of activity.

\*   \*   \*   \*

By now the Soviet agents in Seattle had discovered that the Americans had left a few hours earlier, on a container ship bound for Singapore. Although consummate professionals themselves, they had to admire the resourcefulness the Americans had shown so far, in eluding them.

Major Trsenkov was not happy when he was given the news about the Americans. He had set up his headquarters in a downtown Seattle hotel. Since the death of General Tsoff, he had been reporting directly to one of the Deputies to the Chairman of the Supreme Soviet and had been recently directed to instruct the agents in North America to return to their normal duties.

Because a replacement for General Tsoff had not yet been appointed, agents in Singapore had been contacted directly by the same Chairman's Deputy and given orders to kill the Americans upon their arrival. The agents in Singapore were given the Americans' descriptions, the name of the ship they were on and its expected time of arrival; that was all.

# CHAPTER 8

## Thursday February 18

By early Thursday morning, the ICBM Emplacer-Extractor was in place, straddling the damaged silo. Crews had worked through the night to make sure it would be ready on time. It would still be several hours until the main missile cover's hydraulic control system would be fully operational once again. A base maintenance crew, with the help of engineers from the silo manufacturer, were completing the repairs as quickly as they could.

Hundreds of camp beds had been set up in one of the giant hangers next to the main airstrip and all essential base personnel had been ordered to remain and sleep on the base. Most people on the base only knew there was a problem with the missile in the damaged Bravo Charlie four silo; they had no idea of the extent of the problem.

\*   \*   \*   \*

When Williams and Shelby awoke early on Thursday morning, they could feel that the motion of the ship was very different from the night before. After slowly making their way to the galley, steadying themselves by pushing against the walls along the corridor, they heard there was a storm blowing up from the south-west and less than twenty-four hours into the voyage, a ferocious storm hit. Never having sailed in such rough seas before, both Williams and Shelby became violently seasick. The captain insisted that they go and stand out on a balcony below the bridge, facing into the wind and rain. This was his tried-and-true remedy for seasickness. The men had been given rain slickers and rubber boots and looked like a pair of Boston whalers, as they stood facing directly into the blowing wind and blinding rain. Water was sloshing all around them and it periodically felt as if someone was throwing buckets of water over them. *Some remedy*! thought Williams; it was more like the Chinese water torture, whatever that was. However, with the wind and rain blowing in their faces, they were actually beginning to feel better. They were soaking wet and wondering what was worse - being seasick or drenched from head to foot. The captain had been checking on them periodically and on his last visit, was very pleased when they told him his remedy seemed to be working. He commented to them, in his comical broken English, that they would soon be hardened seaman.

\*   \*   \*   \*

At a very brief ten o'clock conference call with SAC that day, Base Commander Maty told everyone that the countdown variable had been reset again and the nosecone of the missile was about to be removed. He answered several questions about the nosecone removal and then said he needed to leave to go a briefing with Deputy Secretary of Defence Craig and ended the call.

Since Monday, the base commander had been periodically briefing Deputy Secretary of Defense Craig and senior officers from the Department of Defense and the Pentagon. It seemed to Secretary Craig that everything was going well, so he didn't want to interfere and as long as good progress was being made, he didn't see any reason to involve the White House either.

\*   \*   \*   \*

Representatives from the missile manufacturer were focusing on removing the nosecone from the upper stage of the missile. Those on the base who were assisting with the removal were told it was being flown back to the missile manufacturer's plant in California, where they could further investigate a problem with the missile's nosecone. The local contractors had been thankful to get the extra work at this time of the year and had asked very few questions. They really had no interest in the reasons they had been contracted to do the work; they were just happy that they were needed and were being very well compensated.

\*   \*   \*   \*

During a brief conference call with the FBI Thursday afternoon, a senior FBI agent, sitting in for the Deputy Director, told everyone on the call that it had been determined that two men matching the descriptions of the suspects had left Seattle on a container ship bound for Singapore. He said Interpol had been contacted and provided with the suspects' descriptions. Apart from that, he had nothing else to report. As in the meeting in the morning, Base Commander Maty told everyone on the call that the detonation countdown variable had been reset, gaining them another three days.

\*   \*   \*   \*

Late on Thursday, the nosecone was gently lifted off the lower stages of the missile rocket and out of the silo. Although it was swaying backwards and forwards in the wind, it was skilfully lowered onto a concrete skid on the back of a flatbed truck. Following this, forklifts and cranes manoeuvred other concrete sections into place, fully encasing the nosecone. It was being encased to ensure when jettisoned it would drop to the bottom of the ocean. An explanation for doing it wasn't given to those doing the work. While this was going on, the remaining stages of the missile rocket were disengaged from their support systems. The flatbed truck carrying the encased nosecone slowly encircled the base and drove out onto the main runway where a huge B-52 Stratofortress was waiting. A crane lifted the heavy skid off the flatbed truck, onto a special truck, which was in turn slowly winched up into the rear cargo bay into the cavernous cathedral-like interior of the giant aircraft.

*   *   *   *

By late afternoon, the ferocious storm in the Pacific had passed and the sea was calm again. Williams and Shelby were told by some crew members that there were always storms in February during the crossings.

*   *   *   *

It would be late Thursday afternoon before Wolf's truck was repaired.

# CHAPTER 9

## Friday February 19

On the morning of February the nineteenth, flashing beacons were all that could be seen through the darkness as the giant B-52 aircraft lifted skywards. The big aircraft slowly gained altitude and began to fly towards the sparsely populated states of the US north-west. As the plane flew west through one time zone after the next, time almost stood still. The area selected for the detonation had already been designated as a no-fly zone and several United States Navy ships were patrolling in the area.

*   *   *   *

The President had been briefed and was happy with the way things were going, although he was disappointed that those responsible had not been apprehended yet. International protocol required that nuclear tests be announced at least six months in advance and an unannounced nuclear explosion was going to lead to all kinds of questions, in the United Nations Security Council. What the President didn't know was that the Soviets would already know exactly why this unplanned nuclear test had taken place. For them, it would bring closure to the late General Tsoff's failed mission. The President had already decided to explain the unannounced test as being unavoidable due to a malfunctioning nuclear missile - which was actually very close to the truth.

*   *   *   *

On board the B-52 that had taken off from Minot Air Force base, co-pilot Captain Gregory Marks asked, "What time is the detonation planned for?"

"Saturday morning, local time, by which time we should be back at the base," said the pilot, Captain Javier Garcia.

Studying a map, Marks asked, "So where are we heading?"

"Out towards Japan; then, at the International Date Line, we'll head south towards the equator. The drop zone is several hundred miles south of the Johnson Atoll," Garcia explained.

"I see it; you've marked it with an X, south west of Honolulu and south of the Midway Islands."

"Yes, so get comfortable. It's going to be a long haul. I hope you got plenty of sleep last night," said Garcia laughing.

"This sure was a close one!" said Marks. "It really shows how vulnerable we really are, if someone can do this on one of our missile bases."

"Yes. You know, it also shows that no matter how good you think you are doing, it's never enough. I hear that from now on, they're doubling the security patrols along the perimeter of all US missile bases."

"Did you hear if they arrested anyone yet?" asked Marks.

"No, and I was told it is very unlikely they will now," responded Garcia.

"Who do you think did it?"

"Hard to say, but from what I have heard, it seems whoever it was, flew to the base on the way in," said Garcia.

"I heard there was an incident at a border crossing north of the base last weekend," Marks said.

"Yes, they figure it was likely related to the infiltration, but are being tight lipped about it. Do you realize we are among a very small number of people who even know what's really going on?" said Garcia.

At seven o'clock Friday morning, local time, the B-52 and the two escort F-16 fighter aircraft reached the Pacific.

"Only a few thousand more miles to go," said Garcia.

\*　\*　\*　\*

Unbeknownst to Williams and Shelby, while they were playing cards below decks on that Friday morning, they were almost being over-flown by the B-52 on its way to ditch the missile's warheads. Even though it was only their third day out, they had already got into an onboard routine. They would wait until the majority of the crew had finished their breakfasts, then go down to the galley.

There was always lots of food left. After breakfast they would go to the crew lounge and read magazines and books until lunch time, when they would follow the same routine, eating after most of the crew had eaten. Lunch was usually a cold buffet. In the afternoon they would watch a movie. They had watched two Sylvester Stallone *Rocky* movies so far. They had been going to dinner after the crew had eaten and last night found they were eating at the same time as the captain and his officers. He had invited them to his table and seemed to be most interested in both of them. Williams had done most of the talking and had told the captain they both used to work for IBM, being careful not to say where, because they were supposed to be Canadians, and they had recently quit to go on an around-the-world trip, likely heading for Australia first. The captain told them he had been to Australia on a number of occasions and the Aussies who worked on the docks were the toughest men he had ever encountered in any of the ports in the world - and he had been to most of them.

*   *   *   *

At a very brief ten o'clock conference call with SAC on Friday morning, Base Commander Maty informed everyone on the call that the plane carrying the nosecone was on its way to ditch the nuclear warheads, then ended the call.

*   *   *   *

Approximately seven hours after leaving Minot Air Force base, the B-52 had reached its destination. It was seven-thirty in the morning local time. The aircraft was flying quite low, at less than two thousand feet, as the rear cargo bay doors opened. The aircraft climbed and the nuclear cargo tumbled out, end over end into the white-capped sea below. It made a splash as it hit the water and quickly disappeared into the depths below. It would be another twenty hours until the explosion was expected to occur. The huge B-52 gained altitude slowly circled and headed eastward. Captains Garcia and Marks high fived each other, Garcia saying, "Mission accomplished!"

They were both extremely relieved to have successfully delivered their cargo and very happy to be heading for home.

*    *    *    *

That same Friday, Wolf and Carol drove from the northern base perimeter road where Wolf had met the paratrooper coming off the base, to the ski resort, in an effort to try and locate Wolf's hunting rifle. They were now getting close to the ski resort and had not seen any sign of it or anything the paratrooper had thrown into the trees. All the trees they had passed had snow right up to their lowest branches. Carol suggested they should come back in the spring when the snow would be melting and they might be able to find it then. Wolf said it would be rusted by then, so there was no point; he would have to buy another one.

*    *    *    *

At a brief two o'clock conference call with the FBI that afternoon, everyone on the call was informed that the suspects were expected to arrive in Singapore a week from today and Interpol had been formally requested to apprehend them upon their arrival. Deputy FBI Director Harris stated that now that apprehending the suspects was in the hands of Interpol, this would be the last of these daily calls. He thanked everyone and ended the call.

\*   \*   \*   \*

William's plan, which he had already discussed with Shelby, was that once they reached Singapore, they would make their way to Australia. It seemed to be as far away as you could get and he wondered how many other people on the run had escaped to there over the years. As soon as he could, he would get a postcard off to his sister in Sydney, letting her know he and a friend were on their way to visit her and her husband. At least that way she wouldn't be totally surprised when they showed up on her doorstep. He felt confident that he and Shelby would be able to make a new life for themselves there, even though he was still worried that the Soviets would continue to hunt them down. He didn't know General Tsoff was dead.

\*   \*   \*   \*

It was just after six o'clock local time, when the huge B-52 touched down back at Minot Air Force base. The return flight had only taken six hours due to the strong tail winds. Base Commander Maty was very pleased to hear that everything had gone as planned and the warheads were now sitting safely at the bottom of the Pacific Ocean.

News of the successful ditching quickly spread up the chain of command and the President was also very pleased and very confident that he could handle the political fallout following the detonation. He slept well for the first time in a week.

# CHAPTER 10

## Saturday February 20

At a very brief conference call with SAC on Saturday morning, Base Commander Maty told everyone on the call that in six hours from now, the warheads should detonate in the depths of the Pacific Ocean and ended the call when there were no questions.

*   *   *   *

Just after nine o'clock local time in the Samoa time zone, six hundred miles south of the Midway Islands, there was a massive underwater explosion.

*   *   *   *

At four o'clock Saturday afternoon in Washington, the United States government released a statement saying that they had carried out a nuclear test in the Pacific Ocean.

*    *    *    *

Major Trsenkov, now back at the farm, heard the news and knew for sure the mission had failed. He and some of his agents were in the process of putting the farm back the way it had been before it had been rented for the mission. The small light aircraft had already been torn down and its numerous parts buried in one of the unused fields on the farm. He was thinking that there may well soon be another black mark in the KGB's file on him.

# CHAPTER 11

## Sunday February 21

While strolling around the deck of the *Asian Trader* early Sunday morning, Williams and Shelby overheard some crew members chatting about a nuclear explosion in the Pacific.

"Did your hear that?" asked Shelby.

"Yes. It finally makes sense," said Williams, as they walked on.

The captain planned to keep the call he had just had with Interpol to himself. He felt the matter could be dealt with when the ship docked in Singapore. So far, the two Canadians hadn't caused him any trouble.

Williams and Shelby were in the crew's lounge, studying an atlas of the world open to a page that showed a map of the Asian and Australian continents.

"You know, Singapore is right at the bottom of the Chinese mainland," said Williams.

"Yes, I see that. So how are we going to get to Australia from there?" Shelby asked.

"Either by ship or plane. I think ship would be better, just like the one we're on. Security tends to be tighter at airports than at seaports," said Williams.

"I wonder which route ships take when they're going to Sydney?" said Shelby pointing at the map. "Along the top, around and down. Or right down the west coast, past Perth, along the southern coast and up? Either way it looks like you have to go right around Australia to get to Sydney."

"There should be some really good sight-seeing, depending how close we get to the coastline," said Williams. "By the way, don't forget to remind me to send a postcard to my sister."

The captain knew he was breaking shipping company rules by providing the Canadians with a passage. He really wanted to ask them why Interpol was looking for them, but held back, thinking it was better not to confront them in case they reacted violently. He realized he had made a serious mistake allowing them on-board, which could cost him his job, but it was too late to worry about that now. If it came down to it, he would have to come up with a plausible explanation, but he wasn't in the mood to be inventive at the moment.

\*     \*     \*     \*

At a very brief ten o'clock conference call with SAC on Sunday morning, Base Commander Maty told everyone on the call about the announcement by the President the previous day and said he hoped that apart from political condemnation by a handful of world leaders, this would be the end of the matter. He genuinely thanked everyone on the call for all their help and support during the last week and said this would be the last of these conference calls and when there were no questions ended the call.

# CHAPTER 12

## *The following Friday February 26*

Finally the day dawned when Williams and Shelby were due to arrive in Singapore. They were very excited and had risen early on that Friday morning. They were standing on the highest deck of the accommodation block, looking out to sea.

Shelby said, "You know how people wonder how it is that an aircraft made from tons and tons of steel can fly. Well, it's the same for a ship made from tons and tons of iron. You wonder why it doesn't sink like a stone."

"You're right. I've never seen anything made of so much iron as this ship we're on," said Williams.

"It's truly amazing, given how much planes and ships must weigh; it really is quite a phenomenon. It seems to go against everything we know about heavy objects and gravity. Aerodynamics and buoyancy have got to be among the greatest discoveries ever made by man, but you never hear them mentioned."

Just then, the captain put his head around the corner and shouted to them to come and join him on the bridge. When they got there, he handed Williams a pair of binoculars and asked if he could see the dark outline of a long irregular shape far off on the horizon.

"I see it," said Williams, passing the binoculars to Shelby.

Shelby looked through the binoculars just as the captain said, "That's the coast of Singapore off in the distance. I hope you've enjoyed the voyage?"

"Yes, we're hardened seaman now, thanks to you," laughed Williams

Williams shook Shelby's hand and said, "We made it."

"Feels good," said Shelby.

Several hours later, as they were coming into Singapore harbor, Williams knew this would be the time when they would be at their most vulnerable. He figured Soviet agents would be waiting for them. He didn't know that the port of Singapore had been completely closed by Soviet agents who had concocted a bogus story about the *Asian Trader* having to be quarantined due to a serious outbreak of the Asian flu on board. Soviet agents, posing as senior representatives from Singapore's Health Department, had presented a fake Medical Bulletin to the Singapore port authorities, which, among other things, required the complete evacuation of the port six hours before, and twelve hours after, the scheduled arrival of the *Asian Trader* from Seattle.

All incoming road and rail traffic was to be stopped and no other container ships were allowed to enter the harbor. The port authority chairman and harbormaster strongly objected to the closure, indicating that such extreme measures had never been taken before for an outbreak of the Asian flu. They said thousands of tons of cargo would be impacted and they would be contacting the Minister of Health to protest the requested closure. The agent in charge pointed out to them that the Minister of Health had signed the Medical Bulletin, so there was no point in them contacting him or the Health Department. The agent in charge also showed them a fake letter from the Minister of Industry, stating the port authority would be fully compensated for any loss of revenue during the closure. This had calmed the situation.

"Well I guess we have no choice" said the chairman. "We will comply with the Minister of Health's wishes."

The port was cleared of all dock workers hours before the *Asian Trader* was due to dock. No one, including agents from Interpol, was allowed to enter the port. Only the Soviet agents, posing as ministry medical personnel, were allowed to move freely throughout the port.

Soviet agents had been summoned from all over the Malaysian peninsula. Among them were some of the most ruthless Soviet operatives in the world. Life meant very little to them and the death of others even less. Being a Soviet agent in south-east Asia meant that their families enjoyed a better standard of living than most of their fellow Malays, even though they led secluded lives, socializing with only other Soviet-sponsored families. The Soviets took full advantage of the Malay culture of subservience, as even though Malay society was gradually changing, it was still very colonial and a culture that still respected those in authority, who were obeyed without question.

As the huge container ship was making its way towards its wharf within the harbor, there were all kinds of vessel traffic, primarily small craft and coasters, sailing around it. Many of them were criss-crossing in front of the massive ship. From up on the bridge, Williams and Shelby could see a panoramic view of the brightly lit skyscrapers of downtown Singapore through the heavy rain. They left the bridge, telling the captain they were going to get ready for their arrival.

As the ship was coming into its berth, Williams and Shelby were looking over the side at the dark choppy water below. It looked to be very dirty, with streams of green and yellow surface oil illuminated by the bright dockside lamps. The ship's bow thrusters were churning up the dirty water as they helped move the ship into its berthing position. It looked like all kinds of equipment had been readied along the dockside for their arrival; cranes, huge forklifts and large container moving gantries were everywhere, but strangely, they noticed there were no dock workers anywhere, in contrast to the port of Seattle, where they had been everywhere.

As the ship was about to dock, the captain asked his first officer to find the Canadians and confine them to their cabins. The first officer went down to their cabins, but didn't find them there. As he began to make his way down the accommodation block catwalk, he saw them both. He hurried down to where he'd seen them, but when he got there, they'd gone. He looked all around but they weren't anywhere to be seen. He made his way back up to the bridge and reported to the captain that he couldn't find them anywhere. The captain told him to round up as many crew members as he could and search the ship from top to bottom, the fact that his first officer couldn't find the Canadians didn't bother the captain too much. It wouldn't be good for his reputation to be seen assisting Interpol. There was frequently trade in goods other than those that were listed on the ship's official manifest.

Williams and Shelby had got lucky arriving in Singapore on a rainy evening. Seeing no one around, they jumped over the side of the ship, hoping their splashes wouldn't attract any attention. They swam as fast as they could through the dirty smelly water until they reached a concrete jetty. They scrambled up and made their way up a set of concrete steps. Williams peeked up onto the dockside and seeing no one, waved to Shelby to follow him. They ran into the doorway of an old warehouse and stood there, dripping wet, watching the rain come down in the gathering fog. Even though it was raining, they could feel the thick, warm humidity of the tropics. They had made it ashore in Singapore and were now only four thousand miles from the comparative safety of William's sister, in Sydney.

Unbeknownst to Williams and Shelby, Soviet agents were hiding everywhere throughout the port and many of them had seen them run across the dockside into the warehouse doorway.

After several minutes standing in the doorway, Shelby said, "We can't stand here all night; we're going to catch pneumonia."

"Give me a minute," said Williams.

"There doesn't seem to be anyone around," said Shelby.

"I know. Hold on a minute," Williams repeated.

While they had been talking, a huge gantry had been making its way past them.

"Why don't we move along with this big thing?" said Shelby, pointing to the gantry.

"Alright," said Williams, rather impatiently.

They stepped out of the warehouse doorway and moved underneath the giant gantry. It was transporting containers and making a loud squeaking noise as it moved along on top of a set of rusty rails.

Looking up, Shelby said, "Hey, look at the way those containers are swaying right above us! Shouldn't we get out from under here?"

"No, this is an excellent way to leave the dock area. We look like dock workers," said Williams.

"Well, I don't know about you, but I'm scared."

"The gantry operator can't see us, so why are you worried?"

Unbeknownst to them, a Soviet agent was operating the gantry and as it continued to slowly move along, the agent in charge gave the order for the containers it was carrying to be released. As the huge containers thudded to the ground all around Williams and Shelby, they only just managed to avoid them. Williams looked around and noticed that there was gantry upon gantry, lined up along the dockside, all with containers hanging about twenty feet off the ground. It was a trap for sure! Every gantry in the port was in the vicinity of their newly arrived container ship. It was a veritable minefield of hanging containers.

"So what do we do?" shouted Shelby, almost out of breath.

"We need to get away from here. There's something badly wrong!"

Just as Williams said this, shots started to ring out all around them. Automatic gunfire was coming from cranes,

gantries and numerous dockside building windows.
Williams got his pistol out of his backpack and loaded
a new ammunition clip. They could see a train slowly
approaching them from behind and Williams thought
this may also be part of the trap. Hiding behind the legs
of a gantry, they waited for the train to reach them and
began to run alongside it, using it as a shield between
them and the buildings. Williams scrambled up into the
cab of the lead locomotive and pointing his pistol at the
driver, told him to speed up. Shelby scrambled up into
the cab right behind Williams and heard the driver say
he couldn't go any faster because he was getting ready to
take a side track. Gunfire was now being directed into the
cab of the locomotive. The agent in charge was mystified
as to where the train had come from; all rail traffic was
supposed to have been stopped. Shelby could see one of
the monstrous gantries moving towards the train in an
attempt to cut it off. It was clearly on a collision course
with the train.

The lead locomotive that Williams and Shelby were
standing in squeezed past the on-coming gantry, but the
gantry crashed into the locomotive behind, pushing it
off the tracks and down onto its side. Several railcars
behind it and the lead locomotive also eventually toppled
over, falling sideways. Although thrown down, Williams,
Shelby and the driver weren't hurt and managed, with
great difficulty, to climb up out of the locomotive's cab.
Once out, Williams and Shelby ran as fast as they could
towards the train terminal area. Containers were being
released from numerous gantries as they ran under and
past them. The automatic gunfire had started up again
and there was nowhere to hide, except behind the legs of
the giant gantries. A few seconds later, they heard a loud

scream of agony as the locomotive driver was gunned down. Williams managed to clear some falling containers and changing direction, headed for a ramp leading up into a massive container ship.

Shelby wasn't so lucky and got snagged by a falling container. Fortunately, the edge of the container had snared him in such a way that the heel of his boot was taking the weight. Although he was pinned and lying on his stomach, he somehow reached back and managed to remove the lace from his snagged boot. Pulling his leg with both hands, he tried to pull his right foot out of the boot. Bullets were pinging and dinging off containers all around him, making loud metallic sounds. Because his foot was being squeezed within his boot, he couldn't pull it out. He painfully twisted his body around, so he was now lying on his back, rotating his leg in the process. This did the trick and his foot popped loose. He could see row upon row of containers ahead of him and got up and ran towards them. His bootless foot really hurt and he couldn't put any weight on it, so he was hopping along as best he could on his good foot. It was still raining and very dark.

Shelby was wondering what had happened to the gunfire, when suddenly it started up again and he could actually hear bullets flying past his head. Two Soviet agents came around the corner behind him and started chasing after him. He came to the end of a row of stacked containers, turned the corner and ran back in the direction he had just come from. As he was hopping along, he felt something hit him at the back of his right thigh and he stumbled. He felt the back of his right leg and when he pulled his hand away, it was covered in blood. As he hobbled forward, he was hit high on the left shoulder and he went down. The agents who had been chasing him caught up to him.

One of the olive-skinned Malay Soviet agents, standing over him, said, "Do you have anything to say before we blow you away, you American dog?"

Looking up and in pain, Shelby said, "Yes, stop watching so many American movies and get your own lines."

Just as Shelby said this, Williams, who was kneeling about twenty yards away, shot both Soviet agents and they both went down screaming, writhing in pain. Shelby crawled over, grabbed one of their handguns, pointed it at them both, and sarcastically said, "You were saying?"

Williams lifted Shelby up off the ground and they slowly made their way to the end of a row of stacked containers. Shelby's wounds were bleeding badly and Williams could see his jacket and pants were covered with blood. Shelby asked Williams to let him sit down for awhile and Williams helped him down to the ground. He ripped Shelby's pants away where most of the blood was and after checking could see an entry and exit wound; that was a good sign. It looked like a bullet had passed through the outside of Shelby's right thigh, likely causing muscle and blood vessel damage. Seeing more blood on Shelby's left shoulder, he pulled his jacket and shirt down and looked at his shoulder. It looked like he had just been nicked and it was only a flesh wound.

Williams shifted his attention back to Shelby's leg. He took the ripped off pant leg and tied it as high as he could around his leg, cutting off the blood flow as well as best he could. Shelby complained to Williams that he had tied it too tight and he was starting to lose the feeling in his foot.

"It won't be for long, just until I can rig something up around the wound," said Williams.

Williams ripped one of the sleeves off his own jacket. He tied it around Shelby's leg to try and stop the bleeding and to keep the wound clean and then loosened off the tourniquet, much to Shelby's relief.

After Williams had finished with Shelby's leg wound, Shelby asked him if he would look at his foot. Williams could see it was swollen at the back of the heel and could also see a lot of bruising below the ankle. He could see why it would be painful for Shelby to put any weight on it. Williams said there wasn't much he could do for his foot right now.

Shelby was thanking Williams for stopping his leg from bleeding, when they heard voices close by.

"Stay down!" whispered Williams, kneeling down with his pistol cocked.

A Soviet agent came running around the corner. Williams shot him and he went down quietly in a heap. Shots were now being fired at Williams and Shelby from behind and they turned and saw two more Soviet agents running towards them out of the darkness. *Are these people crazy?* thought Williams, as he aimed and shot both of them, knocking them side-ways into some containers. This was five agents he had shot and he wondered how many more of them there were. He took another ammunition clip out of his backpack.

Shelby was looking very pale and was having trouble getting his breath. Williams helped him to sit up, which seemed to help with his breathing. "We need to get you some medical attention."

Shelby just nodded, looking very tired.

"I'm going to carry you," said Williams. "I need you to stand up and lean over my shoulder as I squat down."

Williams helped Shelby to his feet, standing him up on his one good foot. Then he crouched down and Shelby leaned over his shoulder. Williams slowly got to his feet and set off carrying Shelby. All Williams could see were containers ahead of them and they began to hear voices again, which seemed to be off in the distance. Williams was thinking how they could get out from within the containers, even though they were providing cover for them at the moment. He stopped, squatted down and sat Shelby down, leaning him against a container. He climbed up the bars on the container doors of a stack of containers, high enough to peek over the top. Even though it was dark and still raining, he could see they were on the edge of where the containers were stacked and could see the lights from the container ships along the dockside. He jumped down, swung Shelby over his shoulder again and began to make his way to where the container ships were. He was thinking about the men he had just shot, telling himself it was him and Shelby or them - he'd had no choice. As he came to the end of a row of stacked containers, he could see a brightly lit ramp leading up into a container ship. He figured this was the only option they had, so he made his way towards the ramp, shooting out the bright light that was illuminating it. As he was struggling to carry Shelby up the ramp, gunshots started to ring out again and bullets began to ricochet all around them.

Williams turned to see where the shots were coming from and could see flashes lighting up the darkness, high up in the cabs of cranes and gantries. Summoning up all the strength he could muster, he ran up the ramp onto the ship and sat Shelby down on the deck. There didn't seem to be anyone around. Williams knew Shelby needed medical treatment and opened a door at the bottom of the ship's accommodation block. He managed to manhandle himself and Shelby through the door and along a corridor. As they turned the corner, they could see a storage room, which turned out to be unlocked. Once inside, Williams turned on the light and helped Shelby get comfortable, wedging him between some metal buckets. Williams said he was going to see if he could find a medical kit but just as he was about to leave the room, heard voices. He helped Shelby get up, turned off the light and as they were both standing behind the door holding their breath, it opened. Someone looked inside and seeing only cleaning equipment and supplies quickly closed the door, leaving Williams and Shelby standing in the dark. Williams turned the light back on and helped Shelby get into a comfortable position again. Shelby looked like he was getting the color back in his face, which Williams thought must mean the makeshift dressing was working.

Shelby said, "If you find a medical kit, please make sure you bring me some painkillers too; my foot is killing me."

"No problem," said Williams. "I'll bring the whole thing; don't worry."

Not hearing voices anymore, Williams opened the door and looked into the corridor. He couldn't see anyone in the corridor. He shut the door and asked Shelby if he could remember where the medical kits were on the ship they had just been on. Shelby said he thought there was one on the bridge and another in the galley; they were the only places he remembered seeing them.

"Wasn't there one on the wall in the showers, too?"

"I don't remember."

"I think there was. Anyway, that's where I'm heading."

Several minutes later, Williams returned with a medical kit.

"Where did you find it?" asked Shelby.

"In the washroom on this floor, I guess all the washrooms have them too," said Williams. "You know, I think the crew must all be ashore. I didn't see anyone around."

Williams opened the medical kit and there was a box of something called Aspo. He read the information on the side of the Aspo box and it said it was a form of aspirin, only stronger. Williams opened the box and popped out three tablets.

"Here take these; this is what you need. Hopefully you've got enough saliva to swallow them down; if not, I can go and get you some water, if I can find something to put it in."

Shelby quickly swallowed the pain killers.

"Can you lay down on your side?" asked Williams.

Shelby got down on his side and Williams, straddling him, removed the jacket sleeve from around his thigh. The wound looked very clean and uninfected. He wrapped a real bandage around Shelby's leg, covering the wound. Then he looked at his shoulder wound, which he covered with some gauze, secured with strips of plaster. Shelby asked him to check his foot which he said still really hurt. Williams could see it was badly swollen.

"I can bandage it up if you like, to try and give it support." Shelby asked him to do that and Williams strapped it up as best he could with a tensor bandage.

"What now?" asked Shelby, sitting up.

"I think we should stay here for now. You need to rest and I need time to figure out what our next move should be. Try and sleep for awhile," said Williams.

The pain killers were kicking in and Shelby was soon asleep. Williams, sitting next to him, was thinking about the welcome they had just received upon their arrival here in Singapore. It looked as if the Soviet agents had taken over the whole port. Williams hadn't seen one dock worker and wondered how the Soviets could have taken over one of the busiest ports in the world. This was obviously also why no one was aboard the ship except the Soviet agents.

Williams figured that he and Shelby should perhaps wait it out until the crew returned, then make their move, because this would likely mean the Soviet agents had left. Shelby was snoring softly, which seemed like a good thing to Williams. He made some space for himself and using the edge of a mop as a pillow, fell asleep.

Soviet agents were now gathered on the dockside at the bottom of the ramp leading up into the container ship that Williams and Shelby were hiding on. The agent in charge was doing most of the talking, or shouting, which might be a better way to describe it, and was not happy. He was telling the large group of Soviet agents gathered around him that finding the Americans was their highest priority, not looking after the agents who were either wounded or dying among the stacked containers, so none of them were very happy either. He told them to search the ship from top to bottom, because the Americans were hiding somewhere.

# CHAPTER 13

## Saturday February 27

Williams awoke staring down the barrel of a gun. A Soviet agent was standing over him. Williams quickly moved his head out of the line of fire and brought his right boot up between the puny-looking agent's legs. The gun went off and the agent fell on top of Williams, gasping for air, a pained look on his face. Williams hoped no one had heard the gunshot and grabbed the agent's wrist, shaking the gun loose. As he pushed it away, he brought his knee up into the agent's face. Blood started to stream from the agent's nose as Williams pushed him away and stood up, pointing his own pistol at him. He gave the pistol to Shelby, who was awake now, and told him to keep it pointed at their unwelcome visitor while he found something to tie him up with.

Most of the Soviet agents were searching through the rows of containers stacked high on the main deck, but some of them who were searching the accommodation block heard the muffled gunshot, but had no idea where it had come from. They figured that an agent searching between the containers may have fired at a rat, they seemed to be everywhere on the ship.

Williams tied a bandage around the agent's bloodied mouth, making sure he could still breathe through his nose, which might not be so easy now that it was likely broken. Either way, Williams really didn't care. These people were trying to kill him and Shelby, so all bets were off; it was dog eat dog now. He tied the agent's hands and feet together and moved him into a corner of the storage room, under a row of hanging mops and brushes. The room was very cramped now, with the three of them in it.

Williams figured the room was unlikely to be searched a third time, so they should still continue to sit tight until the crew returned. Shelby got comfortable again and fell back to sleep. Williams noticed the Soviet agent was sleeping too and after a while he dozed off also.

Williams awoke with Shelby whispering in his ear, telling him to listen. They could hear voices talking in Chinese. Williams sat up and whispered to Shelby that he would go and see what was going on. Shelby helped himself to more painkillers as Williams was leaving the storage room. He could see the agent still sleeping.

Williams couldn't see anyone in the corridor, so he quickly made his way to the door that led out onto the deck. Once he got out onto the deck, he could see it was beginning to get dark and wasn't raining anymore. He could hear men shouting and the sounds of machinery being operated. Obviously things were getting back to normal again. He went to the side of the ship, looked down and saw a great deal of activity, similar to the way it had been when they were in the port of Seattle.

Someone approached him while he was looking over the side railing and spoke to him in Chinese. Williams nodded and quickly made his way down the ramp leading down from the ship. When he got onto the dockside, he looked around to see if he could find someone who didn't look Chinese or Malay. He could see a big black man driving an oversized forklift and ran over and asked him if he spoke English. Finding out that he did, Williams asked him how he could get to downtown Singapore from there. The forklift operator told him trains left every hour for downtown from the train terminal. Williams thanked him and made his way back to the ramp leading up into the ship. Before walking up the ramp, he picked up an empty clipboard, a pen and a piece of paper, off a table close by. As he walked up the ramp, he scribbled a few numbers onto the piece of paper to make it look like he was working, taking inventory or something. He made his way back to the storage room and when he got inside, told Shelby, who was sitting waiting for him, to take the Soviet agent's clothes. Shelby left the agent, now awake, in his socks and underpants and asked Williams what they were going to do with him.

"Let's leave him here to surprise whoever comes to do the cleaning."

Shelby was limping badly and had to be supported by Williams as they came down the ramp in the gathering darkness. Williams was carrying the clipboard and a handcart, which he had found hanging in the storage room. Shelby was dressed in the Soviet agent's clothes, which only just fit him. He only had one boot on; his right foot was still too badly swollen and he couldn't get a boot on it. Williams's clothes were still very damp from being in the water the night before but there wasn't much he could do about it.

When they reached the dockside, Williams put the clipboard back on the table where he had found it and told Shelby to stand on the handcart. Shelby put all his weight on his good foot while Williams pushed him along the dock, starting to run, making it look like they were playing a game. Dock workers watched them as they ran by, but no one confronted them.

When they reached the train terminal, there were very few workers waiting on the platform. Williams pushed the cart along until they came to a bench seat where Shelby hopped off and sat down. There was a ticket dispenser on the platform which only took coins. Williams figured it must be an honors system, so they would have to take their chances, because he only had large, American dollar bills. They waited about fifteen minutes and a train pulled in. Williams helped Shelby get on board and they sat and waited. There was only one other person in their car and he was reading a newspaper and paying no attention to them. Ten minutes later, the doors closed and the train started its journey into downtown Singapore.

The Soviet agents had left the port late on Saturday morning, after being unable to locate the Americans. One of their agents was missing, three were wounded and two were dead. The wounded and dead had been picked up, but there was no trace of the missing agent. Once he got to his base, the Soviet agent in charge phoned Moscow and told the Deputy to the Chairman of the Supreme Soviet that they had lost the Americans. The Deputy told him to wait for new orders. Not happy with the performance of the Singapore agents, he did not thank him for the information. The Chairman was not at all happy to hear the news and told the Deputy to continue to track the Americans down and kill them. He said their escape was unacceptable because the knowledge they carried must never be allowed to get out.

Soon after leaving the train station in downtown Singapore, Williams and Shelby found a small hotel close by, the Peninsula Mandarin. With Shelby not able to walk far, they figured this hotel would be good. When the hotel clerk asked Shelby what had happened to his foot, he said he had twisted it falling down some steps the night before.

Once they got to their room, Williams removed the dressings from Shelby's wounds and bathed them in warm water. The bullet wound on his leg showed no signs of infection but the flesh wound on his shoulder had quite a lot of redness around its edges. Williams assured Shelby this was a normal part of the healing process. He dried Shelby's wounds and suggested that he leave them uncovered to let the air get to them which should help them heal quicker.

Williams took a quick shower and when he came back into the room, he asked Shelby what his clothes measurement and shoe size was. He said the stores should still be open so he would go and buy them some new stuff. Shelby took some more painkillers and went to bed.

About two hours later, Williams came back to the room with an assortment of jackets, pants, shirts, socks, underwear and shoes. He'd also got some sandwiches, drinks and a bag of ice for Shelby's foot.

After waking Shelby up they both ate, after which Shelby tried on some of the new clothes Williams had bought which fitted perfectly. Williams already knew his fit because he'd tried most of them on in the store.

Williams sat down on the bed next to Shelby and realized he was tired. "Well, I sent a postcard to my sister and tomorrow I'll go and see if I can find a container ship to take us down under to Australia," he said.

Shelby was trying to find a comfortable sleeping position and didn't say anything in response. Williams wrapped the ice pack around Shelby's swollen foot, slumped down onto his own bed, turned off the bedside lamp and was asleep almost immediately and snoring softly. Shelby, still in a lot of pain but feeling groggy after taking some more pain killers, turned his light off and was soon snoring too.

# CHAPTER 14

***Sunday February 28***

Williams woke Shelby up and told him he was going to see if he could find them a passage to Australia on another container ship. He went to the train station, just up the road, and found the port shuttle train platform, where there was a train waiting to leave. Now having some change, he bought a return ticket from one of the machines. When he reached the port, it was very quiet there; he thought it was probably because it was a Sunday. He found his way back to where the container ship berths were and asked one of the few dock workers who was around, if any of them were sailing to Australia. The dock worker said he didn't know; all he knew was that this one they were looking at was bound for Shanghai in a few days. He told Williams to go and check at the harbor master's office. Williams didn't want to do this; he wanted to pay one of the captains again. The harbor master would only tell him container ships didn't take passengers.

He walked up and down the berthing piers, looking at the names of the massive container ships. Nothing jumped out at him, until he came to one named *Pride of Perth*. He figured this had to be Australian with a name like that and looked for a flag, but couldn't see one. There was a ramp leading up into the ship but no one seemed to be around. It looked like the ship was either half-loaded or unloaded; there were cranes towering over it and gantries straddling it. Still not seeing anyone around, he walked up the ramp and looked around on the deck. He still couldn't see anyone and wondered what he should do. He went back down the ramp, sat on some shipping crates and waited.

He waited for about an hour and still not seeing anyone on the pier or on the ship, thought he had no choice but to go to the harbor master's office. When he got there, he found the door locked. Not seeing anyone else around he thought to himself he'd have to come back the next day.

While he was walking towards the train terminal, he saw two Malay dock workers coming towards him. They approached him and asked him what he was doing. He said he was looking for a passage to Australia and asked them if they knew anything about the container ship *Pride of Perth*. One of them said he thought it sailed to a number of Australian cities. Williams asked if it went to Sydney and the Malays said they thought it did. They suggested he should come back tomorrow and check with the passenger lines, because container ships didn't take passengers. Williams thanked them and continued walking towards the train terminal where he caught a train back downtown.

When he got back to the hotel, he told Shelby that he had found a ship that looked like it was going to Australia, but he hadn't been able to meet with the captain.

Shelby said he was feeling much better; his wounds didn't hurt as much and seemed to be getting better and the swelling in his foot had gone down quite a bit since he had iced it the previous night. He also said he was able to get both of his new shoes on.

"That's great!" said Williams. "How about going to get something to eat?"

Shelby said he was feeling very hungry and would like to, so they set off to see if they could find a western-style restaurant.

After walking around the downtown streets for almost half an hour, sweating in the high humidity, all they had seen were food stalls with picnic tables set up in front of them. They were amazed at how unbelievably clean Singapore was; it was spotlessly clean with no garbage anywhere. As they walked around, they stood out from the majority of the short, stocky Malays; they hoped no one singled them out or recognized them. Shelby said his foot was starting to hurt again and he couldn't walk much further, so they decided to eat at one of the cooking stalls. They ordered chicken curry with steamed rice and were given a pot of green tea to take to their table while they waited for the food to be prepared.

As they sat at the picnic table in downtown Singapore, Williams said, "You know, we're pretty close to getting to Australia."

"Good!" said Shelby. "How much money do you have left?"

"At least ten thousand of the Soviets' money and about four thousand of my own. How about you?"

"I have about two thousand pounds and a few dollars."

"I guess neither of us spent much during our training - not really having anything to spend it on, except cheap cigarettes and booze."

After eating the food which tasted pretty good and filled them up, they made their way back to their hotel. Once back in the room, they both took showers to try and cool themselves down in the tropical heat and humidity. Williams told Shelby that tomorrow morning they should check out of the hotel and assume they would be getting a passage to Australia. They were both still feeling quite tired and slept well for the second night in a row.

# CHAPTER 15

***Monday March 1***

Williams and Shelby took the train back to the port of Singapore first thing on Monday morning, crowded in with noisy Malay dock workers. Once they got into the port, Williams led the way to the container ship named the *Pride of Perth.* All the heavy equipment that had been silent the previous day was in full operation. Williams asked one of the dock workers if he knew if the ship's master or captain was onboard and he told him he was. Williams and Shelby walked up the main ramp onto the ship and asked the first person they met where they could find the captain. He told them to wait out on the deck and he would go and call him and asked why they wanted to speak to him.

"Tell him we would like to speak to him about some special cargo we would like him to take to Sydney, Australia," said Williams.

The dock worker went through one of the doors at the bottom of the accommodation block and within a few minutes, returned and asked the men to come with him. Once they got inside the accommodation block, he directed them to a phone hanging on the wall.

"Hello," said Williams.

"Hello, this is Captain Fletcher speaking. I understand you have some cargo you want taken to Australia?"

"Yes, Sydney actually, but I would rather discuss this in person with you, because it's quite unique."

"Wait back out on the deck where you were and I'll be down soon," said the captain.

The captain was a big man, with a thick Australian accent. He shouted to Williams and Shelby as he was climbing down the catwalk on the side of the accommodation block. Soon after stepping down onto the stern deck, he walked over and shook their hands.
He said, "Did you see me come down the catwalk? I like to climb down them sometimes, to see what shape they're in. The ship often gets inspected by the Australian port authorities and my neck is always on the line. Anyway what is this all about?"

"We are the cargo that would like to travel with you to Sydney," said Williams.

"Well, we go there, but why do you want to travel there on a box ship?" asked the captain.

"We are working men, not tourists and will make it worth your while. We already paid for a passage from Seattle to here on a container ship, similar to this one, so we already know the routine."

"You know, this is quite unusual," said the captain.

"We'll pay you four thousand dollars cash," said Williams.

"Is that US dollars?"

"Yes."

"Let me see," said the captain. "I'm pretty sure we have room for you both. Are you ready to go today? We're leaving tonight."

"Yes," said Williams. "We've just got this backpack, no other luggage."

"You boys are travelling light. Where are you from?

"We're from Winnipeg, in Canada," said Shelby, speaking for the first time.

This didn't seem to register with the captain and he said, "Come with me," opening one of the doors leading into the accommodation block. The men followed him up to the second floor where he stopped and said, "Here, you can have these cabins. They have their own shower stall, sink and toilet. I will get someone to give you the keys. Can we settle up, before I take you up for breakfast?"

Williams reached into his backpack, took out a handful of bills and gave them to the captain. The captain counted the money and put it in his back pocket.

"Thanks," he said. "Now let's go eat."

*    *    *    *

Williams and Shelby met a number of the crew in the galley, all Australian. While they were having breakfast with the captain and some of his officers, Williams asked him when they expected to get to Sydney. The captain said the ship would be going to Perth, Adelaide and Melbourne first. He said if the ship left as planned that night, they should be arriving in Perth in a week and should be in Sydney a few days later.

After breakfast, the captain asked a young, tough-looking, member of the crew, called Tony, to get the keys for Williams and Shelby's cabins and to give them a tour of the ship.

Already the accommodations seemed newer and more modern to both Williams and Shelby.

\*　\*　\*　\*

It wasn't long until the Soviet agent in charge in Singapore heard from the Deputy to the Chairman of the Supreme Soviet in Moscow. He was ordered to send agents to all the airports and seaports in Singapore. The Soviet leadership assumed that Singapore was not the Americans' final destination. The agents who had been dispatched to the port of Singapore soon learnt that the Americans had left the day before on a container ship bound for Australia. This information was reported back to the Deputy in Moscow.

The Deputy immediately put his intelligence staff to work in researching the Americans' backgrounds. Within several days, it had been determined that Williams had a sister living just outside Sydney. The Soviets didn't have a very extensive network of agents in Australia but did have a number in each of the large cities.

The Deputy contacted the agent-in-charge in Australia and told him what he wanted him to do. The Soviets plan for killing the Americans had changed significantly after what had happened in Singapore harbor.

* * * *

Williams and Shelby spent most of Monday reading in the lounge, sitting on big comfortable sofas. There was quite a collection of paperback novels on the ship in bookshelves all around the lounge, making it more like a library than a lounge. They found their cabins much more roomy and comfortable than on the *Asian Trader* and figured it was probably because Australians were bigger and required more space than the Chinese.

The next day, Tony joined them while they were watching the shipping traffic sailing around the big ship. He told them they were currently sailing south through the Singapore Strait and would soon be going through the Sunda Strait, between the Indonesian islands of Sumatra and Java. He said this would be in about three hours from now and they shouldn't miss it.

Several hours later, Tony knocked on their cabin doors and told them they were starting to sail into the Sunda Strait and they should come and see it. As they were on their way up to the top deck of the accommodation block Shelby said, "You know, this is already a better voyage than the last one; we didn't see anything except ocean."

"Yes, it's much better when there are things to see," agreed Williams.

They were amazed how close the coast was on either side; they could see hilly jungle-like terrain, dotted with tall palm trees. They were also surprised by the number of off-shore oil rigs in the Strait itself. Tony told them to look over to their right where they should be able to see the remains of a famous volcano. He told them that it was called Krakatoa and when it had become highly active, a hundred years ago, had killed thousands of people and had devastated the whole area. He told them that the Strait was a passage to the Indian Ocean and that they were leaving the Java Sea and the Pacific Ocean behind. Once they had passed by the Indonesian islands of Sumatra and Java, there wasn't much to see for the next few days - just the usual expanse of ocean. The next day, however, Tony told them that they would be passing Christmas Island, which didn't mean much to them. Tony explained to them that the name was interesting because the first explorers, the British he thought, had apparently discovered the island on Christmas Day and thus had named it Christmas Island.

Williams and Shelby followed a similar routine to the one they'd had on the *Asian Trader*. They ate after the crew and spent most of the days reading and watching movies.

# CHAPTER 16

*The following Sunday March 7*

On the sixth day out, Williams and Shelby could see the continent of Australia off in the distance. It was really only an outline and it was not until they were approaching Perth and the port of Fremantle several hours later that they could see the rocky and rugged coastline.

As the *Pride of Perth* was moving into its berth, Williams and Shelby were sitting in the galley; Tony came in and told them they could go ashore with him later that night if they wanted to. Feeling there wasn't much point in sitting in a dock-side tavern, drinking and singing old sea shanties into the early hours of the morning, they both declined, saying they'd found a good movie to watch. Subconsciously, neither of them had been able to get over their experience in the port of Singapore and they didn't want to draw any attention to themselves.

The next day, while containers were being taken off the ship and more were being loaded, Williams and Shelby spent most of the day reading on the balcony of the accommodation block. They were enjoying the sights and sounds of the busy port and watching the large container ships manoeuvring their way in and out of the harbor. The weather was much better in Australia than in Singapore, with warm sea breezes and no noticeable humidity. They were told it was still summer and the temperature was a very warm 85 degrees.

Williams and Shelby repeated the same routine while the ship was tied up in the ports of Adelaide and Melbourne. They still didn't see any point in going to some seedy working man's bar in the dock area. This was not their thing; although they noticed the crew didn't waste any time leaving the ship once their duties had been taken care of. The captain and his officers didn't seem to leave the ship while it was in the harbor. Williams had seen them in the corner of the galley, playing cards and drinking late into the night on several occasions.

Shelby's wounds were almost healed now and he felt no discomfort from them anymore. His foot no longer hurt and the only sign it had been injured was a dark blue line of blood along the bottom.

Williams, always thinking, was wondering what the Soviets were doing to try and find them and wondered if the police authorities were still looking for them also. He figured it would have to be Interpol who would be looking for them now and didn't know too much about them. There didn't seem to be any Soviet or Interpol agents at the port of Singapore on either the Sunday or Monday before they left. He thought perhaps it was a master stroke to be taking another container ship, because this might be the last thing either the Soviets or Interpol would have anticipated.

\*    \*    \*    \*

Interpol were still actively searching for Williams and Shelby, even though their trail had gone cold. On the previous Saturday, when they were allowed to get into the port of Singapore, they met with the captain of the *Asian Trader*. He told them that his crew had been quarantined under false pretences and that the two Canadians had disappeared. He was asked if the Canadians had been confined to their cabins and said they had, but they must have found a way to get out. The captain asked the Interpol agents what the Canadians were wanted for and was told this information was classified. This greatly upset the captain and he said that anything else they wanted to know was also classified and asked the Interpol agents to leave the ship.

The senior agent in the Interpol office in the Singapore reported to the FBI that the suspects' whereabouts were currently unknown at this time. The FBI was not surprised at this, never having had much success working with Interpol in the past. Because the situation had been dealt with, the interest in finding those responsible had waned and it had now become more a matter of national security, than law enforcement.

\*    \*    \*    \*

Life had pretty much gone back to normal at Minot Air Force base. A new missile had been installed in the repaired silo. SAC and Base Commander Maty had made use of the ICBM Emplacer-Extractor while it was still at the base. It was now on its way back to Warren Air Force base in Wyoming.

# CHAPTER 17

*Thursday March 11*

As the *Pride of Perth* was coming into its berth along one of the piers in a large container port, several miles south of Sydney's famous harbor, Williams and Shelby were looking for any signs of anything unusual. It was a bright sunny day and nothing looked out of place. There were dock workers everywhere. Forklifts were shooting along the dockside, and cranes and gantries were in full operation. This was a relief to both of them after their port of Singapore experience. It was now almost a month since they had left Moscow.

They said their goodbyes to the ship's crew and left the deck as soon as the first ramp was moved into place. When they got down onto the dockside, they asked a dock worker if he knew where they could get a taxi. He told them they would have to telephone for one and they would find telephones in the Customs Services building a few hundred yards south of where they were.

When Williams got through to a taxi company, a dispatcher asked him for the address where he wanted to be picked up and the address where he wanted to go. Williams read out his sister's address and looked around and seeing a sign said he was calling from the Port Hobart Customs building. The dispatcher told him it would cost approximately a hundred dollars. Williams said that wasn't a problem, as long as the driver would take US dollars. The dispatcher told him this could be arranged, but there would be a conversion fee. Williams said that wasn't a problem and was told a taxi should be there within fifteen minutes.

Williams joined Shelby sitting on a bench outside the Customs Services building and watched planes landing and taking off from what he guessed must be Sydney airport. As they were sitting there Captain Fletcher and one of his officers came by on their way into the Customs Services building. A short time later, a taxi pulled up in front of where they were sitting and the driver yelled out Williams' name.

As Williams and Shelby approached the taxi, the driver asked, "Are you Mr Williams, for the taxi for Hornsea?"

"Yes that's us," said Williams.

"Jump in the back. Do you have any luggage?" the driver asked in a heavy Australian accent.

Williams said he just had a backpack which he wanted to keep with him. He and Shelby scrambled into the back of the not-so-clean taxi. The driver said Hornsea was quite a way from where they were. Williams acknowledged that this was where they wanted to go and said his sister lived on a street off Junction Road in a place called Waroga.

"You mean Waroongaa," said the driver.

"Well yes, if that's how you pronounce it. It's 26 Derwin Ave, supposedly off the Pacific highway."

"I know roughly where that is and have a map book if we can't find it. You know, I usually work around the harbor area, so this is really going to take me out of my way."

"Don't worry," said Williams. "There will be a nice tip for you. We'll make it well worth your while, if you get us there in one piece. We were told we could give you US dollars; I hope they told you that?"

"Yes, that's alright. It happens all the time, especially around the airport."

The driver asked them if this was their first time in Sydney and they said it was. He told them they were currently south of Sydney, near Botany Bay, where Captain Cook first landed. He said that Hornsea is where two major motorways converge, north of Sydney; it's a nice area, close to a coastal national park.

"Anyway get comfortable. It's going to take us a while to get there."

The driver asked the men where they were from in America and as usual, Williams did the talking. He said they were from Canada, keeping up the pretence, and were taking an extended vacation and coming to visit his sister.

The driver said, "Like most working Aussies, I've never been anywhere, but if I did go somewhere, I'd like to go to Canada."

"It's a big country," said Williams, "but I think Australia is, too, isn't it?"

The driver said it was, but there wasn't much to see in the interior. Williams and Shelby weren't sure what this meant, but didn't say anything.

Williams and the driver continued on a discussion about the two countries for awhile. After about an hour, they had reached Junction Road. The driver pulled over to the side of the road and checked his map book.

"Here it is, just north of here."

When they reached the house, the taxi driver told Williams it would be one twenty, with the conversion fee.

"No problem," said Williams, taking two one hundred US dollar bills out of his backpack and telling him to keep the change.

"Thank you, thank you very much. That is very generous of you!" said the taxi driver. "Here, please take my card. If you need a ride back to the harbor or airport, give me a call. Enjoy your stay in Australia and thank you again."

They knocked on the front door of number 26 and when it opened, Williams' sister greeted them winking and frequently shifting her eyeballs to the right. Based on what she was doing with her eyes, Williams figured something must be wrong. She invited him and Shelby in. As they moved inside, she asked them if they would like something to drink.

"A beer for me," said Williams. "This is Peter, my friend and fellow globetrotter; this is my sister, Sue."

"Pleased to meet you, Gerry mentioned you'd be coming too in his postcard," said Sue.

"Good to meet you," said Shelby.

"Can I get you a drink, Peter?"

"Yes, I'll have a beer too, if you've got one."

"This is Australia; everyone's got beer in the fridge."

Sue returned with the drinks, followed by two clean cut men, pointing guns at Williams and Shelby.

"Welcome to Australia," one of the men said.

"Who are you?" asked Williams.

"We are your Australian welcoming committee. We're going to make up for the welcome you missed in Singapore," said the other man.

William's sister was dumbfounded as she looked at her brother.

"So you work for General Tsoff?" asked Williams.

"General Tsoff, no, he's dead. I guess you didn't hear," said the man who had spoken first.

Williams was trying to keep a conversation going with the Soviet killers. His pistol was in his backpack beside the chair he was sitting in, but there was no way he could get to it. He still had the hunting knife strapped to his leg but didn't know how to get to it quickly. He had to create a diversion of some kind, but how?

"General Tsoff is dead?" said Shelby, not knowing how much he was helping Williams by also engaging in the conversation.

"Yes, he died several weeks ago."

Williams chipped in, "So what have you got planned for our welcoming party and why are you pointing those guns at us?"

"You will find out soon enough," said the agent who had spoken first.

Williams' sister, who was still standing in front of the two agents, put down the tray of drinks on the coffee table in front of Williams and started to step away. All in the same movement, Williams kicked the coffee table and drinks towards the gunmen and pushed his sister towards them. As he slid off his chair sideways, he pulled his knife out of its sheath and threw it. It embedded high in one of the agent's legs. The lead agent pushed Williams' sister aside and fired at him, missing him, as Williams was rapidly crawling towards him on his hands and knees. Williams grabbed his legs and tackled him to the ground; the agent hit his head on one of the upturned legs of the overturned coffee table.

Shelby was also involved now and was wrestling the gun out of the hand of the agent who had Williams' knife sticking out of his bleeding leg. The Australian Soviets proved to be much tougher than the Asian agents. Williams was trying his best to wrestle the gun out the first agent's hand, but could see it was pointing directly at him when his sister came to the rescue and hit the agent directly in the face with a large bronze statue. The Soviet went limp immediately, blood appearing from different parts of his face. Shelby got the better of the second agent and was pointing the agent's gun back at him.

"Are you both alright?" asked Sue. Both Williams and Shelby said they were. "I think I killed him!" she said.

"No," said Williams. "He's still breathing, but he's unconscious by the look of it."

"I need to go to Kevin. He's tied up in our bedroom."

"Go! We're fine," said Williams. "So what do we do with you?" he said, looking at the second agent.

"There will be more agents here soon," the Soviet snarled.

"Not if you tell them we're dead," said Williams. "Do you have a way to communicate with them?"

"By telephone."

"Right then, I'll tell you what. If you phone whomever and tell them we're dead, I won't pull my knife out of your leg and let you bleed to death."

"Yes, I can do that," the agent said, looking down at his leg and at his unconscious colleague.

"Let's wait for my sister and hopefully she can give you a phone to use," said Williams.

Just then Sue and her husband came bursting into the room. "Who are these people?" asked Williams' brother-in-law, Kevin.

"It's a very long story and I'd rather not go into it right now. Do you have a telephone?"

"Yes, in the kitchen."

"Will the cord reach into here?"

"I don't know; I'll go and see," Sue said. She came back into the doorway of the room saying the cord would only reach that far.

Williams pulled the unconscious agent out of the way and helped the other one manoeuvre his way to the doorway.

"What is the number?" Williams asked.

The agent gave him the number and Williams' sister dialled it.

While Williams gently held the hilt of the hunting knife embedded in the Soviet's leg, he listened as the agent told the person on the other end of the line that the Americans were dead and that he and George were leaving. Then Williams whispered to Sue to hang up the phone.

"Good, so now what about you and your friend? What should we do with you?" asked Williams.

"Just let us go. We'll continue to say you're dead. I've already told them you're dead so we can't change our story or we'll be killed," said the agent.

"Just know that if you come back here, you will be killed for sure," said Williams, reaching into his backpack and bringing out his pistol.

Sue and her husband just looked at each other.

Williams asked them if there was a hospital nearby. Sue said there was and Williams asked Kevin if he would drive there so that the Soviets could be dropped off. The agent who had been unconscious was starting to come around.

Williams and his sister's husband bundled the two Soviet agents into his car with Shelby's help. Williams told Shelby to stay with his sister.

When they got to the hospital, Williams pulled the two agents out of the car and sat them down next to Emergency, then reached down and pulled his knife out of the second agent's leg and he screamed out loud. Williams wiped the blood off his knife on the man's shirt and quickly ran and jumped into the car and told Kevin to floor it. He looked back and could see someone standing talking to the two wounded men.

Once Williams and his brother-in-law got back to the house, Williams sat him and his sister down and along with Shelby, told them as succinctly as he could why these men had tried to kill them.

"So these were Soviet agents?" said his brother-in-law.

"Yes, but I'm pretty sure this is the last we will see of them. As of right now, my friend Peter and I are dead as far as the Soviets are concerned. Now how about that beer?"

"Yes, I think I'll have one too," said Sue, getting up and moving towards the kitchen.

Kevin just sat looking at Williams and Shelby with a wide-eyed stare.